THE
MOTHERS

Angeline Trevena

Bogus Caller Press

ISBN: 978-0-9934864-3-2

Cover art: Ben Farrow
Cover art copyright © 2017 Ben Farrow
www.estragonhelmer.com

Published by Bogus Caller Press
www.boguscallerpress.co.uk

Publisher's note:
The Mothers is a work of fiction. All names,
characters, and places are the product of the
author's imagination, used in fictitious manner. Any
resemblances to actual persons, places, locales,
events, etc. are purely coincidental.

ALSO BY ANGELINE TREVENA

Cutting the Bloodline

The Paper Duchess Series:

The Bottle Stopper

The Matching

The Visionary

FOR MY BOYS

With the end of all things,
come a million different possible beginnings.

THE HEAD

THE KEEP

THE EYE

NEWSTONE

THE WILLOWS

THE BAYS

THE BEECHES

THE BIRCHES

HAVERHEAD

THE CLIMB

THE LAWNS

HEIGHT STREET

SALT STREET

THE GARDENS

LYNSTOCK

BUCK WAY

FORGE STREET

BRIDGE LANE

THE STEPS

HOPE STREET

SILK LANE

WASH STREET

THE WATCH

SATIN SQUARE

FOLD STREET

THE LADDER

DUTIES

SECOND STAIR

THE HOPE

TOP STREET

INLET ROAD

EXIT ROAD

THE COMPOUND

CRICK LANE

COMPOUND STREET

NAVEL STREET

THE HIDE

THE DOWNS

HIND STREET

NON LANE

EYE STREET

HUNG STREET

OVERLOOK

TONGUE STREET

OVERLOOK

THE WALL

THE WALL

THE SLIP

THE FLOOR

POLL STREET

THE EDGE

DOWNSIDE

THE CUBES

THE CUBES

THE SQUEEZE

THE EDGE

FALWERE RIVER

1

Tale wiped her damp forehead with a floured hand. It was too hot in the kitchen. Its wide windows always caught the afternoon sun, and it warmed like bread in an oven.

She looked down at the lump of pastry in front of her. The fruit pie filling had been bubbling happily on the stove, filling the house with a sweet and spicy scent, but she felt suddenly sick. The heat was making her tired and turned the homely smell into an unwelcome stench.

As she lowered herself into a dining chair, she grabbed a towel and mopped her face with it. This was not what she had imagined her life would become. Domestic. Blissful domesticity. Freda would have laughed.

Tale closed her eyes. She hadn't thought about Freda for a very long time; she always caught the memories before they had a chance to root, and locked them away even tighter. Her brain was like an over-packed suitcase, in danger of springing open if she were jolted too hard. And those memories jolted her.

The front door clicked open, and Tale sat upright, her hands automatically moving to smooth down her hair.

Colby came straight into the kitchen. "Hello, darling." He bent and kissed her gently on the cheek. Always on the cheek. He understood that anything more made her uncomfortable, and he was kind enough not to push the issue.

Tale gestured helplessly towards the pie. "I wanted to have it ready for tonight, but it's too hot in here. I needed to sit down for a while."

Colby smiled, his lip sitting crookedly where he was missing a tooth. "Don't worry about it, I'll finish it. Why don't you go for a lie down?"

"I'm tired of lying down. I want to hear about your day. Remind me that there's still an outside world."

Colby's laugh was light, childlike, and completely at odds with his broad shoulders and bulky arms. He laughed generously, especially when he was nervous or unsure. Tale's constant discomfort seemed to leave Colby unsure a lot of the time. He deserved better, but Tale couldn't offer him any more. Not yet.

He turned his back to her, and set about rolling out the pastry.

"It was just a standard day really. We're looking at more streamlining strategies, which means more potential redundancies. I hate that bit of my job, choosing who to lay off. It's unfair. How can anyone make a decision like that? Still, that's the world of business I suppose. We're not running a charity. It's all about cost-cutting and increasing profits..."

Tale closed her eyes again and let herself drift carelessly on the sound of Colby's voice. She didn't care what he was saying, she just needed to hear someone talking.

She opened her eyes and looked up at him. He had turned around, his face expectant.

"Sorry, what?" she stammered.

"Are you even listening to me?"

She felt her face flush. "I'm sorry, I was just enjoying the sound of your voice."

"You don't have to stay holed up in here all day, y'know. It's not like you're sick."

"What am I going to do? Pop down to the community centre and join a knitting circle? Swap stories about how useless our husbands are?"

He laughed again. "You might enjoy it. How do you know if you don't even try? I don't mean talking about how useless I am though."

"Behind locked doors I'll be the perfect little wife for you, but please don't make me do it in front of other people."

"I know, I know. It will ruin your tough-girl image, eh?"

"If I wasn't so exhausted I'd beat the hell out of you right now."

Colby laughed. That sound made this place home. She could bake as many pies as she liked, but it was him that turned this building into a place she could imagine spending the rest of her life. Actually imagine being happy.

"More of my men have been moved down to The Hope," Colby said.

"They're moving more down there?"

He shrugged. "That place is nearly empty now, and Lynstock is jam-packed. They're living like sardines here."

"I can't imagine what that would be like. Living alongside unmarried men."

"There have been a lot of attacks. The women on The Hope aren't safe anymore."

"Any safety they thought they had was nothing more than an illusion. Women will never be safe here."

"Don't you feel safe?"

Tale looked up at him. "At least I'm not waiting to find out what kind of man I'm going to belong to."

Colby waved a hand at her. "I don't own you. You'd never let anyone own you, and I wouldn't want to anyway."

"I'm lucky I got you."

"I hope so."

Tale braced her hands on the table and pushed herself up to standing. "Maybe I will have a lie down after all."

"Good. I'll come and wake you when it's time to eat. Can I bring you anything?"

Tale shook her head.

As she passed by Colby he reached out and placed his hand on her rounded belly.

"Be kind to your mummy, stop making her so sick and tired all the time, you hear me?"

Tale smiled up at him. "I don't think he's paying

any attention to you."

"I guess I'd better get used to that."

Tale looked down at the floury hand print on her dress. "There's a lot we still have to get used to."

2

Minnie flexed her hand before curling it into a ball and knocking sharply on her supervisor's door. She'd approached and run away from his office six times already.

After a moment, his voice came back. "Come."

The door stubbornly opened over the thick carpet, and Minnie stepped onto it, conscious of the footprints she'd likely leave. Evidence of her presence.

Jarrett was leaning back in his chair, his legs slung up on the desk, his socks a pale brown between his polished shoes and pressed trousers. He was all about appearance, setting a good first impression. But it was all an illusion. He was laid back and, while lazy was an inappropriate word, he was certainly economical with his efforts. Quiet and mild-mannered, he was the kind of man any woman would hope to be paired with.

"What can I do for you?" As he spoke, he shifted his feet to the floor and leaned forward. He had a way of making people feel like they mattered.

"I was wondering if I could get a pass to visit The Hope."

"You've been working here for almost three years now and you've never requested a pass. What's the special occasion?"

Minnie felt the heat rise into her cheeks. She'd known that he'd be suspicious, but the blush wasn't going to give her away as a liar; in fact, it worked quite well with her cover story.

"I have a date," she said quickly. "I wanted to get something nice to wear."

Jarrett grinned. This was no longer a supervisor talking with a subordinate, it was co-workers gossiping.

Minnie's face was so hot she was sure her cheeks would blister. "Hector," she muttered.

"Really? I didn't think he had it in him to ask out a girl like you."

"A girl like me?"

"Well, you are rather headstrong."

Minnie automatically dropped her eyes to the floor, although she sensed no tone of reproach in his voice.

"It is, of course, my duty to remind you that as a ward of the administration—you know what that means—they own you. And any husband will have to be approved. I'm sorry, you know I'm just fulfilling my duty as your supervisor."

"I know. But it's just a first date, I'm not exactly thinking about marriage."

"Good, I wouldn't want to lose you yet. Look, you know that I'm just... you know..."

She looked up at him with a sigh. "Just doing your job."

"For what it's worth, I approve."

Minnie offered a hint of a smile. She didn't even think of Hector romantically, but the inescapable truth of her situation as an owned woman left her feeling bitter.

"And as a show of good will," Jarrett continued, "you'll find some extra luxury credits in your pay packet this week. Buy yourself something special, eh?"

"Thank you."

"You deserve it. You work hard, and you're damn good at what you do. You know how rare it is that a woman's allowed a job. It's not permitted readily, she has to truly excel. Make herself indispensable. You run rings around any man here. If I could, I'd promote you over them every time."

Minnie nodded. She knew all too well that her nose was squashed against the glass ceiling. She was more than qualified for a more superior role, but women weren't allowed to rise to management level. Not in Falside.

"I appreciate the thought, sir."

He nodded and lifted his legs back up onto his desk. "Well, back to work." He winked at her before closing his eyes.

Backing out of the room, Minnie gently pulled the door closed. She barely even realised that she wiped the handle clean with her sleeve.

Turning, she followed the steps down to the Main. She glanced around. The officers were idly leaning against the walls, waiting. The Mother was quiet, her body limp against the pipes. Doped up for now.

Turning her attention towards the control rooms, Minnie spotted the back of Hector's head, his white coat draped over his narrow shoulders. He was still awaiting delivery of a coat that actually fitted him. She'd have laughed if she wasn't so nervous.

Balling her hands into fists, Minnie walked through the open door and gently cleared her throat.

"One sec," Hector said, his face bent close to the screen he was inspecting.

Minnie waited, hoping that her nerve would hold out. "Hector..." she offered.

"One sec," he repeated, sharper this time.

She tapped her toes against the tiled floor and glanced up at the high ceiling above her. For a moment, she considered running away, maybe back to her room, hiding under her bed covers, pretending to be sick with something horribly contagious. Then she considered smuggling herself out of Falside somehow. Perhaps she could dig a tunnel, or build a rocket, or—

"Sorry Minnie, I had to concentrate. What can I do for you?"

Minnie looked up into Hector's expectant eyes, and swallowed down what felt like a tennis ball.

"Hello Hector, working hard?"

"Always."

They stared at each other for a moment.

"Did you want something?" Hector asked.

"Umm, yes, of course." A dribble of sweat made its way down her spine. "I was just wondering if, perhaps, if you're not doing anything else, or, indeed, seeing anyone else. I mean, I didn't want to presume that you weren't, you might be, it's just that we've never talked about that stuff before, not that I can't imagine another girl, or boy for that matter, I...I'm rambling, aren't I?"

Hector nodded. "A little."

Minnie took a deep breath and closed her eyes. "I wondered if you wanted to go out for dinner with me."

There was a moment of silence, during which Minnie realised that her eyes were still screwed shut. She opened them.

Hector was smiling. And blushing. But, most importantly, he was smiling. "I'd love to," he said.

3

"Tell me again," Maeve demanded.

Harris dropped his head into his hands. "Haven't you heard it enough times already?"

"If you keep telling it, you might remember something you didn't before. Something that seemed insignificant."

He sighed and looked up at her. It was hard for Maeve to see her father like this: his face was thinner, his cheekbones like razors trying to break through his skin. His eyes were tired, faded, and cradled in cavernous sockets. He'd been washed, shaved, and had his hair cut, but the time he'd spent as a prisoner of the administration was all too evident. He'd fill out soon enough, especially with the amount of food the sisters were forcing into him, but his eyes would be changed forever.

Maeve looked down at the table between them.

"I'm sorry, I just… I need to make sense of it."

Harris smiled bitterly. "That's exactly what I've

been trying to do. I just think there is no sense to be made."

"Let me just get it straight in my head. You had no warning, no expectation, no idea you were going to be released?"

Harris gave a big sigh. "Maeve, sweetheart, I'm exhausted, and I've told you this story so many times already."

Maeve gripped the edges of the dog-eared journal that sat on the table in front of her.

"There really is only one explanation," she said with a nod.

As she opened the journal, the pages fell apart at the right page. She'd looked at it hundreds of times. She dreamt about it. It was imprinted on the backs of her eyelids. Running her fingers over the paper, she could feel the indentation of the words. Corinn's name over and over. At least, that's how she read it.

"I really don't think this girl, Carolyn, had anything to do with it. They just had nothing to hold me on."

Maeve tried to discard it, but the thought had already crept into her head. And before she could stop it, it dropped from her mouth. "You see, you got her name wrong. Maybe that's what she does; gets people to forget her. It's how she's stayed undiscovered for so long." Maeve shook her head. That seemed to be happening more and more often.

Harris leaned forward and lowered his voice. "Maeve, you're really starting to sound like a crazy person now."

Her eyes flew up to meet his. "You think I'm crazy?"

"We're all just worried about you."

"Worried about what? I'm fine. I've got you back, and everything is falling into place. Just like Mum said it would."

She closed the journal and ran her hands over the cover.

"I've finally got something to focus on, something to strive for, and everyone thinks that makes me crazy."

"That's not it. But this journal's become an obsession. You must know every word of it by heart." He cleared his throat. "It's becoming more important than the things that should be your priority."

"My whole life I've had to live without my mum. Finding my own way, teaching myself, looking after myself. Now I finally have something of her, a real link, and you want to take that away from me?"

"You're neglecting yourself." He scratched his head. "You're neglecting Faith too."

"I am not. And don't forget that you're the one that took my mum away in the first place."

"I haven't forgotten that. How could I possibly forget that? But Faith is filthy, and miserable. And whenever she comes here, she eats like a horse. Are you feeding her properly? You're meant to be her mother. She should be your priority."

Maeve stood up, her chair screaming back across the floor. "How dare you? You've not even been here for the past four years. I've raised her all alone. I'm practically still a child myself."

"Then let us help you."

Maeve folded her arms.

"Leave her here for a few days. The sisters are more than happy to look after her. Sort yourself out."

"So, what; you've all been plotting this behind my back? You think I'm an unfit mother."

"We just think you need to take some time to yourself. Have a break."

Maeve snatched up the journal. "I don't need a break. I think I'd like to take my daughter home now."

"You looking after her was only ever meant to be temporary."

"Faith!" Maeve yelled up the corridor. Her throat was tight, forcing her voice into a screech. "Faith!"

"Mummy?"

Maeve looked up and spotted the girl, crouched halfway up the stairs. She clung tightly to the skirts of one of the sisters.

"Come on, we're going home," Maeve said to her. "Now, please." Walking to the foot of the stairs, she held her hand out. "Come on, Faith, now."

Faith looked up at the sister and then back at Maeve.

"Faith, come on." Maeve caught sight of her father leaning against the kitchen doorway. She couldn't let him be right.

"Maybe she should stay here for a bit," the

sister said.

"I would like to take my daughter home. Faith, get here now."

Faith looked at her with eyes that had filled with tears. "Mummy?"

"Faith!" Her demand came out harsher than she had intended, but she couldn't back down. She couldn't let them take everything away from her.

Faith looked up at the sister, and slowly rose to her feet. Her hand was still knotted in the skirt. "Mummy's angry."

Maeve stopped, her hand frozen on the bottom of the banister, her foot poised to ascend the stairs. Her heart was a rock, sinking down through her body, leaving her chest an empty cavern. She moved back, slowly, as if retreating from a wild animal without spooking it.

It wasn't Faith she saw sitting on those stairs, terrified. It was her. And if she'd glanced into a mirror, she was sure she'd have seen Uncle Lou staring back.

The tears came fast, surprising her, and the violent sobs brought her to her knees. But there were arms around her, and gentle words, and maybe she hadn't become the monster that her uncle was. Maybe things would be alright.

Through the tears, Maeve nodded. "Faith can stay here," she gasped. "I need some time."

Harris' hands eased the journal from her grasp. "Why don't you leave that here too?" he said.

Maeve half-heartedly tried to cling onto it, but part of her wanted to burn it, or toss it into the river.

She nodded again.

Harris pressed his lips against the top of her head. "Take some time to get your head straight. We all care about you. We all love you. When you're ready, we'll be here."

4

It was strange, being outside of The Eye, and Minnie took detours around groups of people, wrapped her hands up in the sleeves of her cardigan, and kept her eyes focussed on the ground. Falside felt immense, and noisy, and intimidating.

One of the other women, Bianca, had offered to come with her, but Minnie had managed to put her off. Even if she hadn't been planning a secret rendezvous with Kerise, she wouldn't have been able to bear spending the day with her. Minnie knew nothing about Bianca, she wasn't even sure which department she worked in, because she never talked about herself. She filled every silence with inane babble and endless questions, but always managed to steer the conversation away from focussing on her. Minnie could never trust someone like that. In fact, few of the women there did. Minnie had heard rumours that she was a spy. But then, there were always rumours about someone. Even Minnie hadn't been immune to the finger of suspicion when the conversation grew stale.

The Hope wasn't how Minnie remembered it. She'd been brought there a few times as a child, and the image she held was some kind of utopia for women. She couldn't help but grin at her naivety now. The situation was clearly far worse than the administration admitted.

Stopping on Inlet Road, Minnie found herself looking directly into The Hide. She could see part of the screen, mounted above the square—cycling the same adverts, selling the same ideals—and she could count the women on her fingers. There were so few that they looked like anomalies, oddities. Minnie was used to being acutely aware of her gender, of being part of an extreme minority, but seeing the same imbalance out in the world was a shock.

She had been right that something was going to break, but it looked like it would be happening sooner than she had thought.

Men crowded the space once owned by women. They lounged at café tables, they idled in and out of the shops, they ate, they drank. They were at home here. Even the businesses around the square had changed; the traditional coffee shops now selling beers and burgers, windows previously filled with dresses now boasted trousers and jumpers, suits, leisure equipment. Frills had made way for functionality, and the last feminine domain had disappeared almost entirely.

The security of seclusion was gone too. The

few women were huddled together in twos or threes, arms linked, heads close together, as if being female had become a secret only shared with closest friends. For a brief moment, Minnie wished she had Bianca by her side.

Officers patrolled in pairs too, heavily and visibly armed, their gaze roaming back and forth over the crowd like oscillating fans.

This had been a mistake. However suffocating it was, The Eye was a sanctuary. She was untouchable there. She had a status more than simply meat.

She could feel the eyes on her like hands; every man that walked past, casting his gaze the full length of her body. Weighing her up. Pricing her up. She was watched in The Eye, constantly, but she wasn't looked at.

Glancing behind her, she took note of the men there. Two officers, three smoking, four moving around, one staring. She made quick assessments: could she outrun them? Could she fight them?

Bowing her head, Minnie moved on towards The Hide. There were women there, and she supposed that she could find safety in numbers.

An arm linked into hers and she jumped. A girl, younger than herself, smiling at her as if they were old friends.

"You shouldn't walk out alone," she whispered.

Minnie patted the girl's hand on her arm. "Thank you."

"Although, of course, you're not exactly alone."

"What do you mean?"

The girl cocked her head slightly, just the ghost of a motion. "Those two officers have followed you all the way down here. Either you're in trouble, or you're someone special."

"Aren't all of us women special?"

The girl laughed. "More so every day I suppose."

They walked in silence for a moment, slowed, and came to stop in front of the screen in The Hide.

"Can you remember the last time they announced the birth of a girl?"

Minnie shook her head.

"Almost a year now." She gasped. "Did you hear about the baby that got snatched?"

"No."

"Straight out of the pram. The mother was stood right there, looking into a shop window." She lowered her voice. "Being a good little consumer. They dress their girls in blue now. Keep their hair short."

"Did they get her back?"

"Oh yes, she was found within a few hours."

"What happened to the person who took her."

The girl smiled grimly. "What do you think? The poor woman had seven boys of her own at home. Seven. Imagine that. Desperately trying for a girl."

"And how safe are we?"

"Well you're very safe, with your own personal guard. Seriously, who are you?"

"I'm no one," Minnie replied.

"Maybe you've been picked. Must be someone important."

Minnie frowned. She'd never even thought what it might be like to be married off to a stranger. She'd always known that the administration would have to approve any potential husband, but to have a man choose you, and to have no choice at all in the matter.

"In fact," the girl continued, "I'm surprised you've not been married off already. I'm getting married in a month. I'm fifteen years old."

Minnie's hand flew to her mouth. "No. You're a child."

The girl shrugged. "Not anymore. I'm a wife. A breeding machine. Just like the woman who took that baby. Desperately trying for a girl."

"We need to change it."

"What can we possibly do?"

Minnie didn't have an answer.

"Maybe I'll be lucky, eh? Maybe my husband will be kind."

Minnie smiled weakly. "Yeah, maybe."

"I'm Celia, by the way."

"Minnie."

"So, where did you want to go today, Minnie?"

"Where's good to buy a nice dress?"

Celia grinned. "I know just the place."

They walked on in silence, out of The Hide and up towards Crick Lane. Every building along here was a brightly lit shop, alternated with narrow doorways that led to the apartments above. The street was filled with people. Married women and single men, occupying the same space, but that was where the connection ended.

The women hurried along in small groups, their eyes fixed on the floor. Most of them wore hats or scarves, and some also wore veils; a gauze covering eyes or entire faces. Despite the warm weather, they were bundled under several layers and bulky coats. They were there only out of necessity, and moved on as soon as they could.

In comparison, the men lounged in doorways, drinking, smoking, gambling. They wore their shirt sleeves rolled up, and concealed their roving eyes behind dark glasses. They were completely at ease. This was their territory now.

Minnie followed Celia through the crowd, dodging one way and then the other, deftly moving through the throng.

Towards the end of the road, where it narrowed, they finally slowed and stopped in front of a shop window.

There were no clothes on display like in the other windows, just drapes of deep red velvet. The folds of material flowed from the top of one corner, down across the floor, and finally pooled around the claw feet of a delicate gold-coloured chair.

"What is this place?" Minnie asked.

"A little-known gem. Come on, I'll introduce you."

A tiny bell chirped as they opened the door and stepped into the dim interior. The small space was crammed with overflowing racks of clothing. The walls were covered in dark blue flock wallpaper, and the woodwork was painted to match. Every available surface was crammed with mismatched lamps, their shades adorned with fringes.

An elderly man appeared through a curtain at the far end of the shop. His body was twisted, his gait stiff, but the eyes behind his small glasses shone with vitality. He smiled broadly, and opened up his knobbly arms to embrace Celia tightly.

"How's the blushing bride?" he asked.

Celia uncoiled herself from his grip. "Barely blushing at all." She gestured towards Minnie. "This is Minnie. Minnie, this is my grandfather."

He stepped forward and offered a set of gnarled fingers for shaking.

"Valentine," he said. "Pleased to meet you."

Minnie shook his hand gently, fearing she might break off a digit like a twig from a tree.

"It's nice to meet you too."

"What can we do for you today, Minnie? A bridesmaid's dress perhaps?"

He winked at Celia who replied with a scowl.

"I have a date," said Minnie. "I need something nice."

"A date?" Celia asked.

"Er... with my parents," Minnie corrected. "It's an important thing, my dad's work. I've been instructed to look nice."

Valentine nodded knowingly. "Something conservative then?"

"Something modern," Minnie added.

Valentine thought for a moment, his brow pleated. "Right. Yes." He glanced Minnie up and down, and turned to a rack of clothing. The clothes hangers squeaked along the pole as he flicked through them. He muttered to himself as he did so, reasoning every decision, every rejection.

Minnie glanced at Celia who returned a reassuring smile.

The dress Valentine finally pulled from the rack, with a very definite nod, was a soft, pale blue. The bodice was overlaid with a crochet camisole, below which a gathered waist gave way to a full skirt that rippled and flowed like water. The straps were thin; daring and provocative.

As if reading her mind, Valentine gestured to another rack. "You can pick out a shawl or a shrug to go with it. What do you think?"

Minnie stepped towards it, her fingers reaching out. "It's stunning. Perfect."

"Try it on," squeaked Celia, hopping up and down.

The changing room was an alcove covered with a curtain; deep red velvet. As Minnie undressed her elbows bumped repeatedly against the walls, and she wished she were a little more elegant. It was what the dress deserved. As she pulled it over her head, she silently apologised that she was nothing more than a clumsy, awkward nerd of a girl, about to embark on what would probably be the most painfully humiliating date anyone had ever had.

The skirt dropped around her legs, and hung in even, perfect drapes. Squinting, Minnie dared to raise her eyes to the full length mirror before her.

At first, she thought it was a trick, some kind of illusion. Minnie turned from side to side, letting the skirt swell around her. The reflection twisted too, following her every move. She moved faster, trying to trick it, trying to prove it wasn't her. Because it couldn't possibly be. As she spun once more, she stumbled. She smiled up at her slightly embarrassed reflection. It was still her in there. She may be dressed up, but she was still that clumsy girl more at home in a lab coat.

"Come out," Celia's voice came through the curtain. "We want to see."

Minnie took a deep breath, counted to three, and pulled back the curtain.

Celia gasped, her hands covering her mouth, and Valentine nodded knowingly.

"You look amazing," Celia whispered.

"I'm not really sure it's me."

"It is, it is, it's totally you." Celia rushed forward, grabbed Minnie's hands, and spun her around. "It's definitely you, and you look gorgeous."

Laughing, Valentine took hold of Celia by the shoulders. "Don't get her all dizzy now. Let's get that dress wrapped up."

As Valentine boxed up the dress, along with a shrug in a matching pale blue, Celia danced around the shop in excitement.

Valentine leaned forward and whispered to Minnie over the counter. "You'd think it was her buying a new dress for a date."

"You would."

"So, who's the lucky man?"

Minnie blushed. "It's for my parents' party."

"Yes, of course." Valentine rolled his eyes.

"Getting forgetful."

Minnie pulled her purse from her pocket, and slid a collection of credits across the counter.

Valentine unfolded them. "Administration-issued credits, eh?"

Minnie glanced over her shoulder. "Aren't all credits issued by the administration?"

"Yes, but these ones are only issued to the women on their payroll. I've only ever seen them once before."

Minnie stared at the floor, her cheeks burning.

"Don't worry, I'm not going to tell her." He pushed the dress box towards her. "I just don't want any trouble coming to her."

"No, it won't, I promise. She's been so kind." Minnie looked over at her. "A true friend."

"Enjoy your date. I hope he deserves you."

Minnie smiled. "Thank you so much." Tucking the box under her arm, she walked to the door and pulled it open. The bell chirruped above her head.

"See you soon, Celia darling," Valentine called as they stepped back onto the street.

Opposite, two officers watched them pass. Minnie risked a backward glance. They were following.

She tapped Celia's arm. "Thank you so much for taking me to your Grandfather's shop, but I'll be fine now. I'm just heading home."

"I'll walk you."

"No, really, I'm fine."

Celia stopped and turned to face her. "To be honest, it's been nice to have someone to talk to. I live alone in a three bedroom house here. The houses on either side of mine are empty. I've never been so alone."

Minnie took hold of Celia's hand. "And I wish things were different, so that we could be friends. But I don't want to get you into trouble." She tilted her head by the tiniest of angles, gesturing towards the officers.

"You aren't just one of us, are you?"

Minnie sighed. "I don't want to get you into trouble. The best thing you can do is to keep your head down, enjoy your wedding, and try to be a good wife."

"My husband is thirty eight years old," Celia whispered. A tear made its way over the curve of her cheek.

"I'm so sorry that the world is like this."

Celia shrugged. "I've never known anything else."

"You might soon. Just hang in there. I have a feeling things are about to change."

"How can you be so sure?"

Minnie smiled. "You'll just have to trust me. When it's all over, I'll come and find you."

"What's going to happen?"

"I'm not even sure. But stay safe. When all this is over we can..." she searched for an appropriate phrase, "hang out."

Celia snorted. "I'll hold you to that."

Minnie squeezed her hand tightly before letting go.

Rather than heading back to The Hide, Minnie

turned right towards Second Stair. Searching the crowd, she saw a familiar face.

Kerise raised an eyebrow in question. Minnie shook her head tightly. Just the tiniest of movements. She flicked her eyes to the side and watched Kerise focus her gaze on the officers that followed. As they passed, their hands brushed.

"Not safe," Minnie hissed.

"Soon though," Kerise replied.

5

Kerise turned towards the buildings and pushed her way out of the main flow of people. She watched Minnie walk away from her, their opportunity lost. Then she watched the two officers pass her. Her own private guard. The administration really were jumpy.

It was frustrating though, having to put their plans on hold once again. They'd spent too much time putting things off, waiting for the right moment. There'd been too many setbacks.

Things were getting desperate. It was obvious to see. The overflowing of single men from Lynstock, the increase in attacks on the few women left. Things could only get worse.

And to finally have her daughter back, her precious Minnie, who she never imagined she'd ever see again. To have her so close, but to still be out of reach was a new level of suffering.

She kicked at the wall beside her, achieving nothing by it. She would have to be patient. Again.

Pulling her hood back over her head, she dug her hands deep into her pockets and wandered up towards Second Stair. Someone bumped her, and she muttered an apology, but made no more acknowledgement than that. Her brain felt like a sandcastle being washed away by the sea.

As the shops of Second Stair gave way to the terraced houses of Top Street, Kerise looked up, and brought her focus back to her surroundings. She'd been walking blind, and deaf, and unprepared.

She stopped. Ahead of her, Tale stopped too. Their eyes held one another's for a moment, before Kerise dropped hers to Tale's swollen stomach, a protective hand cupping its curve.

Tale smiled awkwardly, and shrugged. Kerise nodded in greeting. And then the crowd carried Tale away.

Pregnant. Tale was married. And pregnant.

6

The bell above the door jingled cheerily, but it still sounded foreboding to Maeve.

The sisters moved as one, like a caterpillar, crawling from behind the counter, to block the door to the rest of the house.

"Maeve," the sisters chorused. They drew her name out, and somehow turned it into an accusation.

"Where's my dad?"

The sisters looked at one another.

"Upstairs," one of them said.

"With Faith?"

They looked at each other again before nodding in unison.

Maeve took a step forward, and the mass of hips and breasts fortified.

"Come on, let me through. I've not seen Faith for three days."

"Are you sane?"

"Am I sane? Really?" Maeve held out her arms and turned around. "Do I look crazy?"

The sisters mumbled.

"I'm perfectly fine," Maeve insisted. "Let me through."

Reluctantly, the sister creature relented, arms flailing in resignation, and Maeve pushed her way through the fleshy bunting of their underarms.

She hauled herself up the stairs two at a time, avoiding the spaces where the edge of the stair or the banister rod had been worn smooth by her constant sitting there. She doubted that this place would ever get rid of Uncle Lou's ghost entirely. Not for her, at least.

Somehow, Harris already knew she was there, as he intercepted her on the landing.

"Faith's sleeping," he said, grabbing Maeve by the shoulders. He turned her around and marched her back down to the kitchen.

"What is this?" Maeve demanded. "I'm not even allowed to see my own daughter now?"

Harris slowly shook his head.

"Go on, say it," Maeve said.

"Say what?"

"That she's not my daughter."

He turned to look at her. "I wasn't going to say that at all. You've more than earned your right to call her that. It's just that I was hoping you'd be calmer. More rational. You don't seem ready to have her back yet."

Maeve sighed. She let that sigh pass right through her. "You're right. I'm sorry. I guess I came here expecting the worst, and my behaviour is making that come true. I'm sorry. I'm calm."

Harris eyed her. "You just seem a little—" he searched for a word "—frantic."

"Frantic." Maeve sat down at the table. "I can't disagree with that. I think a few days apart have been good for us. You were right. I needed that."

"I hope you're not just saying what you think I want to hear."

"No, no, I really feel it. In fact, you want to know how much I mean it? You can keep the journal. There. I don't want it back."

Harris sat opposite her. "About the journal. I was reading through it, and I came across some things that made sense to me. They probably made no sense to you though."

"Like what?"

After a moment of simply staring at the table, Harris finally continued. "Premonitions, I guess. Ones that came true."

"Will you show me?"

Harris looked at her then, and she could see the doubt on his face.

"I'll still let you keep it," she said. "You can be the Keeper of the Journal."

He nodded. Leaning his chair back onto its two hind legs, he pulled open a drawer and produced the journal.

Maeve tried to feel nothing when she saw it, but her fingers ached to touch it, her eyes longed to roam over its pages. She forced the surge in her chest back down, and set her face to neutral. How had she let this book take such a claim over her?

Harris laid his hand over its cover. "Just

remember, this is not your mother. This isn't messages direct from her to you. They're ramblings, echoes. Some woman heard voices and wrote them down, it doesn't mean they're all from Selene, or, in fact, that any of them are. You understand that, right?"

Maeve nodded.

As Harris flicked through the pages she leaned forward. She was able to identify each page from just the briefest glimpse. He stopped and smoothed the journal open.

"Here."

Maeve looked where he was pointing. She knew the phrase well, another puzzle to be solved.

Raise the dead. She can't see, she can't see, but he'll take her eye because he loves another.

"What does that mean?"

Harris frowned. "You don't need to know. But it relates to me. That premonition was right. And this one." He turned a few pages.

She can't escape. She'll die as you watch, and there's nothing to do. Hearts break, and little ones never get the chance to breathe.

"That's about me too."

"And I guess you're not explaining that one either."

"It doesn't change anything. The point is that these things happened. These messages came true."

"So you believe me, that these are messages from her?"

Harris closed the journal and folded his hands over its cover. "I'm not saying that. I'm saying that there is some truth in here, that's all. Someone foresaw these things, but we can't possibly know that it was Selene."

"But it could have been."

Harris shrugged. "It could."

Maeve smiled. "That's good enough for me."

7

Tale slowly laid herself back, and rearranged the pillow under her head. Looking up at the tiled ceiling, she tried to relax. She closed her eyes, but Kerise's face was there. She flicked her eyes open again, and pushed any thoughts of Kerise out of her mind. Because with thoughts of Kerise, thoughts of Freda inevitably followed. She had to concentrate on her baby right now.

"Can you uncover your belly please?" the sonographer asked.

"Oh, sorry," mumbled Tale. She lifted her hips and gathered her skirt up over the swell of her stomach. With her legs uncovered, she felt exposed and vulnerable. And thankful for the darkness in the room.

"This will be cold."

The tube of gel farted, and Tale fought the childish urge to laugh. She felt so tense, the situation was so alien, and a bout of uncontrollable giggles sat in her chest like a stone.

The sonographer ran through his checks like a

mechanic doing an engine service. He measured the baby's skull and the number was nothing more than that to him. He checked the organs, the limbs, the spine. It was business. Routine. Not a tiny, actual person whose arrival would change Tale's life in unknowable ways.

"Everything looks good," he said finally. "A healthy little baby. I'm just going to confirm the sex."

Tale held her breath.

Leaning forward, the sonographer pulled the curtain closed between Tale and the screen, blocking her view. Women weren't allowed to know the sex of the baby anymore. Many had died or been left unable to carry children after seeking out illegal abortions to get rid of an unwanted boy.

The probe was pushed deep into Tale's stomach, and she inhaled sharply. As did the sonographer. Tale was sure of it.

"All done." The curtain tore back, and Tale looked straight at the screen. It was already blank.

The sonographer smiled and nodded towards Tale's belly. "Take good care of that one." He handed Tale a wad of paper towels.

"I intend to." It seemed to take forever to clean the gel from her belly—there was so much of it— but she was desperate to get out of that room. The air was suddenly thick, she could barely swallow it. She tugged her dress down, and it clung to her sticky skin.

"Are you all right getting home by yourself? Perhaps I could call your husband for you?"

"I'm fine. He's at work." Tale backed away.

"I'm sure he wouldn't mind. It's just one phone call, it won't take long."

"Really, I'm fine. It's not far." She pulled the door open and almost tripped out of it.

"It won't take a minute," he called after her.

Taking a deep breath, she followed the toilet signs down the corridor, her head spinning.

The tiled toilets were cool, and after washing her face, Tale felt a little more stable. She looked into the mirror and inspected her tired eyes.

"That was weird, right? Was he a bit *too* concerned about me?" she asked her reflection.

"Yes, that was weird," her reflection confirmed with a nod.

"Then I'm not completely paranoid?"

Her reflection thought it over for a moment. "Maybe not completely."

"Then, do you really think...? Do you really think this could be...?"

Her reflection didn't respond, but her aching bladder did, and Tale hurried into a cubicle.

On the inside of the cubicle door was a poster showing a happy couple cradling their baby. It wore a pink hat, was wrapped in a pink blanket. Nothing like pushing the point home. The poster claimed that 'every child is a blessing', but it was clear what the real message was.

She pressed her palms into her eyes and winced. "C'mon girl," she mumbled.

As she washed her hands, she avoided eye contact with her reflection, instead preoccupying herself with soaping every inch of skin.

She wandered back down the corridor, where a group of staff were gathered behind the maternity reception desk, heads together, with the sonographer. They glanced up at her, nudging and shushing one another.

Tale pressed the button for the lift and waited.

"Is that her?" one of the nurses whispered.

"Yeah, that's the one."

"But look at her, she's nothing."

"I spotted it," the sonographer said.

The others muttered in agreement, patting him on the back, shaking his hand as if he were the proud father himself.

8

Maeve flicked back the curtain on the small window set into the front door. Squinting back at her was an officer, the peak of his cap pulled low, skimming his eyebrows. It was the badge he wanted her to see, not his face.

"Just a moment!" she called, and scuttled back to the bedroom.

She crouched down to Faith, and took hold of her small hands.

"It's time for you to climb into the wardrobe, darling, just like we practised. Remember? Small and quiet. Just like a little mouse."

"Mummy, I don't like it in there."

"I know, darling."

The officers hammered on the door again. Maeve winced.

"Please, sweetheart, just for a little while."

"Mummy, no."

The heavy knocks came again.

"We don't have time to mess about, Faith." Grabbing her by the hand, Maeve tugged Faith to her feet, while she pulled the wardrobe door open with the other hand.

"Mummy," Faith whined, pulling backwards.

"If you don't get in there right now, Mummy will be arrested, and we'll never see each other again. Is that what you want?"

Faith clambered into the wardrobe and crouched down in the darkness.

"Remember," said Maeve, "you have to be quiet."

Faith raised a shaking finger and pressed it against her lips as tears ran down her face. Fighting back her own tears, Maeve pushed Faith further back, and placed the wooden board in front of her, shutting her into a secret compartment. It was dark, it was cramped, it was lonely. But it was the only way to protect her.

Maeve pulled off her cardigan and scooped Faith's toys under the bed with her foot.

The officers hammered at the door again. "Officers! Open up!"

"Alright, alright," Maeve called. She unbolted the door and pulled it open. "I was sleeping, I wasn't dressed," she explained, as she put her cardigan back on.

The two officers were young, their brand new uniforms still crisp, the buttons not yet smudged with fingerprints. But their demeanour didn't match their smart appearance. They were distracted, bored maybe, their eyes roving around, their shoulders slumped. They'd probably drawn the short straw on jobs today.

One scrolled through his screen. He frowned. "Maeve Richards?"

"Yes?" Maeve did her best to try to sound impatient.

"You're a difficult woman to track down."

"I'm a busy woman. What do you want?"

"We're here to register you for your ID bracelet. It's so that you can access services such as—"

"I know what it's for," snapped Maeve, cutting him off. "I don't need the spiel. Keep your propaganda to yourself. I know what this is really about."

The officers looked at one another with a smirk.

"Are you the only one here?"

"Yes."

"The neighbours mentioned a young girl lives here."

Maeve's heart hammered so hard she was sure the officers would hear it. "No. That's my niece. She's already registered at her own address. I take care of her sometimes."

One of the officers nosed past her into the house. Maeve resisted the urge to shut the door in their faces, and instead, pushed it open wider.

"Did you want to have a look around?"

Their boots dragged the mud of the slums in with them, trailing it across the floor in streaks. Maeve would be scrubbing them later. Unless they found Faith, of course.

She held her breath as they nosed about. The kitchen, the bedroom, the bathroom. There weren't exactly many places to hide.

One officer bent and peered under the bed. He dragged out one of Faith's toys.

"My niece's. Like I said, I look after her."

He stopped by the wardrobe. The door was slightly ajar. He pulled it open with the tip of his finger and looked inside.

Maeve willed Faith to keep quiet. Even the slightest sound could give her away. If she moved, or sobbed, or even breathed too loudly, they'd both be arrested, and dragged up to The Compound. She could only guess at what might happen after that.

The house, the whole of The Floor, seemed to become unusually quiet.

The officer sniffed, nodded, and turned away from the cupboard. Maeve slowly exhaled, keeping her breath silent.

"Ok?" he said, catching the second officer's eye.

"Yeah, ok."

"Right arm please."

"What?" said Maeve, taking a step back.

"Right arm." He unhooked a contraption from his belt, a thick stick with a claw at one end. He smiled. "Don't worry, it looks worse than it is. It won't hurt, I promise."

Slowly, Maeve raised her arm. The officer opened the claw and laid Maeve's wrist inside it.

"It goes with a bit of a bang," he said. "But try not to flinch, and do not pull your hand away. You wouldn't want to lose it, would you?" He laughed.

Maeve glanced at the wardrobe door, still slightly ajar. She closed her eyes.

The claw snapped closed around her wrist and she jumped.

"All done. See, completely painless." He pulled the claw open again, and Maeve looked down at the ID band that now sat snugly around her wrist. She felt sick, and she wanted them out of her house.

"Here." The officer held out a pamphlet. "It tells you everything you need to know about the bracelet and the services you can access up on The Hope."

"Great, some bedtime reading."

The officer curled his lip. "Enjoy." And then they were gone.

Maeve moved quickly; bolting the door and tugging the panel free from the back of the wardrobe. Faith uncurled from the cramped space and instantly wrapped her arms around Maeve's neck, nuzzling her nose in.

"I'm so sorry sweetie, I'm so sorry you had to go in there."

"Please don't make me hide again. I'll be quiet."

"Oh darling, it's not because of anything you've done. It's because you're special, and there are people who want to take you away from me. But I'll never let them, ok?" Maeve wiped Faith's wet cheeks with her thumb. "I'll never let anyone take you away from me, ok?"

9

Instead of heading home from the hospital, Tale's feet led her somewhere else. Somewhere they knew well, somewhere she didn't even realise she was going until she was there.

The small window was ajar, as it always was, but the broken crate she used to climb on had been replaced with a small stool. She'd asked Denver so many times for something more sturdy to stand on, worried she'd fall and break her neck, and he'd finally done it. But was he waiting for her return, or was there someone else using this entrance now?

Either way, she wasn't going to fit through that gap now.

The alley at the side of The Paper Duchess was crammed with crates, bottles, food waste, old clothes, and, remarkably, discarded books. Books with broken spines, torn covers, burnt edges. Their pages were scattered across the ground; words among the weeds.

Tale frowned, and pushed her way through,

with her hands braced against the wall on either side.

The front of The Paper Duchess was impressive; with tall pillars flanking the large, wooden doors, and the domed roof visible above. It was almost intimidating. Tale took a deep breath and walked up the few steps to the front door. She couldn't remember if she'd ever used this entrance before.

The air was cool inside, the sheer size of the room denying even the sun to warm it. It tried though: elongated strips of light chequered the room, silhouetting the tall window frames across the stone floor. But to no avail. Tale's breath expressed as steam, and the skin on her arms pimpled.

It wasn't how she remembered it. Everything was ordered, tidy, catalogued. It was a proper bookshop now, no longer the disorganised mind of a madman. It was quiet, pensive. Creepy.

She walked along by one of the shelves, drawing her forefinger along the ridge of spines. Like one long backbone. She thought of the tiny spine curled inside her belly, and her hand instinctively settled on it.

Turning, Tale looked over towards the bar. The last time she was here, she had been desperate. So desperate that she was willing to lose her hand for the woman she loved. She couldn't even recognise that person anymore. Or those feelings. Her world had fallen apart that day, but she had rebuilt it. Although, here she was; returning to her past when she should only be thinking about the future.

Footsteps started their way up the back corridor, paused, and then continued. Tale glanced at the front door. Could she escape before anyone saw her here? Could she pretend she was never here at all? She twisted, but her feet refused to move. And then he was there. Staring at her. Mouth open.

"Hello Denver," she said.

His mouth moved, but no sound broke forth.

"I guess this is a bit of a shock then?"

His eyes roamed down to her stomach, and his jaw worked even harder to force out some words.

Tale patted the bump. "Yep, I'm a married woman now. Doing my bit for the good of the city."

Denver finally closed his uselessly flapping mouth, and stepped forward, wrapping Tale into his bony arms. "I've missed you," he whispered. "So, so much."

"I've missed you too."

"I thought you hated me," Denver said.

"I did. I didn't." Tale broke free from his tightening embrace. "I was hurt, angry, confused. It was easiest to hate you for it. To blame you. But when I calmed down and I could finally see what your part really had been in all this, too much time had already passed. I thought you'd be angry at me. I was scared. I thought I'd lost you forever. I kept telling myself I'd come and see you tomorrow. Then weeks had gone by. Then months, years. I'm sorry."

"No, I'm sorry. I should've come and found you."

"No, it wasn't your responsibility." They looked at each other before snorting with laughter.

"This is silly," said Denver.

"As are we."

"So what brings you back now? Why is today different?"

Tale shrugged. "Ask my feet. They were the ones that brought me here. And I'm really glad they did. My stupid pig head was never going to do it."

Denver pulled her back in for another hug. "I'm glad they did too."

He held her for a while, and they just breathed against one another. Tale could almost forget that life had moved on, that so much had changed forever. Maybe if she stayed here just a little longer, she could go back to her home on Top Street, and Freda would be there. Still lazing in bed. Her hair spread across the pillow, bright red in the sunlight. Just maybe.

But Denver was already pulling away, and the illusion fell away with his arms.

"Can I see the room?" she asked.

"Sure."

She followed him through to the corridor beyond and wandered down a few doors before stopping. Denver reached for the door handle, but Tale snapped out her hand and placed it over his.

"Wait a second."

"Is it all a bit too weird?" he asked.

Tale nodded. "Like a really intense déjà vu. But

from some kind of parallel life." She took a deep breath. "Ok, I'm ready."

As she removed her hand from his, he twisted the handle and pushed the door open.

The smell hit her first. Beyond the musty dampness of a room that's not being used, came the familiar scent of cabling, electricity, computer parts, and coffee. She could smell paper, the ink from the printer, the worn cushion on the chair. The entire room reached her nostrils, recreating itself in aroma. She closed her eyes. She could almost smell Freda too. The scent of her shampoo, her talcum powder, her lipstick.

Tale stumbled, and grabbed the door frame. Denver's arms were around her again, lending his strength. "It was too much. You should sit down."

He led her into the smell of the room, wafting it all around her, and sat her down in her own chair. Her own desk. She looked up. Her own computer. Everything exactly as she left it, awaiting her return. And here she finally was.

The keyboard was so familiar under her fingers. The dampened click of the keys. More like a gentle thud. Like a punch to the gut.

Tale whipped her hands away, and pushed them between her knees.

"Are you alright?" Denver asked. "Is it too much?"

"It's just..." Tale shook her head. "Memories, y'know."

He nodded in reply.

"And what is this anyway? Some kind of

shrine? Why haven't you packed it all up?"

Denver shrugged. "I guess I was just hoping that you'd come back. That everyone would. Freda, Kerise. That things could be like they were."

"That's the one thing they can never be."

"I know. It was just a comfort. I was lonely."

"Denver, I'm so sorry." She took hold of his hand. "I should have come sooner."

"It doesn't matter now. It was silly really I guess, just me clinging onto the past."

"And me trying to deny it."

"Did it work?"

Tale smiled grimly. "Did it work for you?"

"Hardly."

Tale looked around the room. It was strange being back here. Like returning home, but with nothing being the same as it had been. It was like walking into your house and feeling like someone had been there, even if there's no physical evidence of them. Just an uneasy feeling. Just something not quite right. A violation. That's what it was. But the trespasser was her. She didn't belong. Not anymore.

The chair lolled backwards as she stood up, stumbling onto its broken wheel.

"I need to go."

Denver squeezed her hand. "Please don't."

"I can't. I can't be here."

"Tale, please. Can't you just stay for a bit? I could make us coffee. You could fire up the computer. It might still work."

"And what, Denver?"

"Maybe we could do it again. Start up Asteria. Look, you've had loads of letters. They've never stopped coming."

He grabbed a box from under the desk and dropped it into her chair.

Tale picked up the top envelope and turned it over in her hand. She dropped it back down.

"I can't. I'm married now. I have responsibilities. It's not just me anymore."

"We'll be careful."

"It's far too dangerous. And what if we get caught? Besides, I can't exactly climb through the back window anymore, can I?"

"I'll put a door in for you."

"An unregistered door?" She shook her head. "No, Denver, this isn't my life anymore."

"So what, you just live happily ever after and let whatever happens happen?"

"My husband's a good man. I can make this work."

"You're just going to give up? Live the life they prescribe? Where's your fire gone, Tale?"

"I never had any fire. That was—" She clamped her mouth shut.

"Freda? Say her name, goddammit! What would she think of what you've become?"

Tale stared at him. "Why should I care what she'd think? She chose to leave."

"I'll tell you what, she'd bloody hate it. She'd hate that you'd given up."

"I haven't given up. I just have different priorities now, and leading a revolution isn't one of them. I have to protect my baby."

"Why would you want to bring a child into this?"

"This is the only world we have."

"And once upon a time, you wanted to change it."

Tale threw her hands into the air. "And what did we achieve, Denver? Everything's the same now as when we started this."

"But it can be different."

"Can it? You know what hurts more than anything? The broken dreams. The false hope. I will not break her heart letting her believe in something that will never happen."

Denver stared at her, breathing hard. "Her?"

Tale looked down at the fullness of her belly. "Yes. Her."

"Lots of women think they're having girls. It's just another 'false hope'. Your words."

"No. I had a scan today. I heard them talking. I'm having a girl."

Denver stepped back, his eyes glued to her stomach. "A girl." He gulped. "And how do you feel knowing what her fate will be?"

"Terrified. It terrifies me. Especially because I know there's nothing I can do to change it."

10

They were barely through the door before Faith ran over to the sisters and threw herself into their awaiting arms. She was devoured by bosom, smothered by chins and cheeks and lips.

Maeve crossed to the counter and climbed onto one of the stools. She wondered how her life might be different if she'd been so fervently loved.

One of the sisters looked down at Maeve's arm.

"They got you then," she said.

Maeve scratched at the ID band. "They had to eventually."

"And Faith?"

"I kept her hidden."

The sisters sighed as one.

"But The Floor isn't safe for us anymore. It's crawling with officers every day now."

Three chins nodded. "They're here almost daily checking on our women. Making sure they've all got bands, double-checking details."

"What do they want with slum girls?"

"Isn't it obvious? Even slum girls are better than none. They've started to talk to the women about moving up to The Hope."

"You're kidding."

"They've got lots of empty houses, and lots of empty cots at the hospital. Those things need to be filled by someone."

"But they can't just...kidnap women."

A finger came out of the sister creature and tapped Maeve's ID band. "How much choice did you have about that? They can do whatever they want, love."

"But that means...that I...that Faith." Maeve reached out and grabbed Faith's ankle, gently tugging on it. "We need to get out of here."

"And go where?"

Maeve didn't answer. She couldn't. If it was no longer safe on The Floor, where could they ever be safe? They couldn't live beyond the reach of the administration anymore. They were right under its eye, and that eye was wide open.

Faith giggled as the sisters tickled her, her legs kicked uselessly at the mass of stomach.

"You alright here for a bit, sweetheart?" Maeve asked her.

She nodded in between bursts of laughter.

Maeve eased herself down from the stool and weaved through the tables to the door that led to the rest of the house.

It was quiet, and Maeve took a moment, sitting down on the bottom step, and closing her eyes. Her hand went to her wrist, her fingers running around the circumference of the ID band. She was caught, trapped, like an animal with a wire nose tightening around its neck. She couldn't lose her daughter. Faith was everything.

There had to be a way out. The supply routes; by road, or via the river. But she had no money for bribes, and she wouldn't know who to ask anyway. Even if it was safe. There were stories, of course, of women getting out, but there were so many more of them getting caught, and shot.

A creak at the top of the stairs opened Maeve's eyes and turned her head.

"Hey," Harris said, smiling broadly. "I didn't mean to disturb you from your thoughts."

Maeve shrugged. "No bother, they weren't happy ones anyway. You need the left side of that step to avoid the creak."

"Thanks for the tip. So why the unhappy thoughts then?"

Maeve held up her wrist.

"Oh God, they got you."

"It was inevitable."

"Where's Faith?"

"With the sisters. I managed to keep her hidden. This time anyway. But we need to get out of Falside."

Harris shook his head slowly. "There is no way out of Falside. Not for women, at least. I heard they're shipping men out by the bus load. Putting them to work on farms and plantations further out. There's just too many of them for Falside to cope with now."

"Is it true that they're moving slum girls onto The Hope?"

Harris cocked his head from side to side, weighing up his answer. "It's what people are saying. I stopped in at the monastery earlier, and Grant said they haven't seen it happen, and they haven't married a slum girl yet, but there's talk. But then, there's always talk, so who knows?"

"So what do I do? Is there somewhere you can hide us? Some safehouse somewhere, now that The Floor's no longer safe for us."

"I only had that one house, where you stayed with Faith before, but The Hope is the last place you want to be. That is, if they haven't reclaimed it to house more single men."

"You know what will happen if they find Faith, don't you?"

Harris came down the rest of the stairs and sat next to her. After a moment, he put his arm around her shoulders and pulled her against him.

"I wish I had a solution for you."

"I do too."

11

Kerise dropped from her perch on the wall into the garden below. It was small, but tidy. The lawn was closely clipped, the expanse of it broken by agreeable shrubs and neat flowerbeds. Clustered by the back door were large tubs that made up a kitchen garden; tomatoes, bell peppers, onions, herbs. It was the perfect image of the domestic ideal.

The back door was unlocked, not that it would have presented much of a challenge otherwise.

The warm kitchen beyond was bright and tidy. No dirty pots, no discarded dishes, no piles of food waste. Something sweet was baking, and the smell of it flooded saliva into Kerise's mouth.

After opening a few cupboards, she found a tin of small, neat cakes topped with just enough butter icing to be a treat, without it being ostentatious. Everything here was so carefully controlled, rationed even.

She popped one into her mouth and sucked it for a moment, and the sticky, soft flesh of it moulded to the roof of her mouth.

She sat herself down at the table, folded her hands in front of her, and waited.

After just a minute or so, a timer buzzed somewhere in the house. She heard the creak of furniture, the groan of a pregnant woman waking, and then slow, sluggish footsteps towards the kitchen.

She smiled as Tale yelped.

"Hello, big mumma," she said.

Tale staggered backwards, her hand balled into a fist at her chest, full of the fabric of her dress.

"Jesus, Kerise, you scared the bloody life out of me. I'm pregnant. You have to be careful."

Kerise leaned over and looked at the floor. "Don't fret, I've not broken your waters."

"What the hell are you doing here?"

"Sampling your cakes." She nodded towards the open cupboard.

"Actually, Colby does most of the baking. He's tried to teach me, but he has some kind of magic touch with it."

"Yes, they're very good. Is the little allotment out there his too?"

"Mmhmm, he's always talking about extending it."

"Likes things neat and tidy, eh? Just so."

"What do you want, Kerise?"

"Can I not just pop round to see an old friend to congratulate her on her happy news?"

"Yeah, because that's just your style, isn't it? I suppose you've organised a surprise baby shower too, huh?"

Kerise held her hands up. "You got me. Unfortunately, no one else wanted to come, so it's just me. And I didn't bring you a present either."

"Don't go into business as a party planner, will you?"

"Damn, that has been my dream for such a long time now."

Tale turned to the oven and pulled the door open. Slipping on an oven glove, she lifted a dish out and placed it on a cutting board.

Kerise sat up. "That smells good. What is it?"

"Apricot crumble. Did you want some?"

"Hell, yes. Dish that up."

Tale grabbed two bowls from a cupboard and served up two portions. She placed them on the table with a couple of spoons, and sat herself down.

"Look at you now," Kerise said. "The perfect little wife."

"I'm trying to be."

"For whose benefit?"

"My husband is a good man, Kerise. He's kind and gentle and thoughtful. He treats me really well. He deserves a good wife."

"And being a good wife means abandoning everything you've ever believed? Everything you've fought for?"

"Yes. In Falside, yes it does."

"So you're willing to set aside your own life, just to please a man who bought you?"

"He's a good man."

Kerise leaned forward and eyed Tale closely. "Are you in love with him?"

Tale gasped. "No! I like him, a lot. Maybe. I don't know. Where did love get me the last time?"

"At least you actually felt something with Freda."

"Don't say her name in my house."

"Have you forgotten her so easily?"

"No, Kerise. Nothing about this has been easy. But she chose to leave, that was her choice. She left me."

"Because she loved you."

"Love? That wasn't love. At best it was an infatuation. A bit of youthful rebellion. A 'fuck you' to the system."

"You felt it strongly enough."

"We all do when we're kids. And that's all we were. But I can't play make believe anymore. Love is sacrifice, and compromise, and something that's just there. It's not running around with your heart on fire the whole time. It's not something that you should feel like you're constantly fighting for. She was the one that left, Kerise, and I was the one left behind with all these feelings and nowhere to put them. And everyone acts as if I'm the one that's lost my damn mind just because I'm hurt and angry. I'm allowed to feel things, and, goddammit, I'm allowed to express those feelings however I want. Just because you disagree with me doesn't make the way I feel any less real. Or any less important for that matter."

"At least you've still got some fight left in you."

Tale grunted. "All of my energy, all of my 'fight', if you want to call it that, is for me and my baby now. Not some pipe dream, not some valiant cause. You might still want to be a hero, I just want to be a good mother."

"And a good consumer, and a good little breeder breeding the next generation's workforce."

Tale jabbed the tabletop with her finger. "You have your cause, your higher purpose, and that's fine, but mine has changed, and you need to respect that."

"I would if I really believed you. You know that all of this is wrong. It's an illusion that's breaking apart at the seams. This isn't sustainable. What chance does your son have of ever marrying or having children? One day, there will be no more generations of children. What happens to the world then?"

"I don't know."

"Not your problem, huh? Well it'll be your son's problem."

"I didn't say that I didn't care, I said I didn't know."

With a squeal of her chair, Kerise stood up and began pacing the kitchen.

"You should go," said Tale. "Colby will be home soon, and if he found you here—"

"He'd be angry?" Kerise interrupted. "He'd yell, throw things? Punch you about a bit?"

"God, Kerise, why does every man have to be a monster?"

"Because their system has made every woman

a victim."

"Colby didn't invent the system."

"But he supports it. Look at all this. This perfect little home, perfect little wife, perfect little baby. Urgh, he couldn't be more of a model citizen if he tried. It makes me gag."

"If we're so unworthy of you and your rebellion, what are you even doing here?"

"I came to ask you to come back. I want you to write Asteria again."

Tale was already shaking her head before Kerise finished talking. "Not a chance. It's too dangerous."

"It was always dangerous."

"And I didn't have anyone else to think of then. I have responsibilities now, people who rely on me. It's not like it was."

"But it can be. You just need to say 'yes'."

"No. Those days are behind me. I have way too much at stake now."

"Your family will die with him," Kerise said, pointing at Tale's belly. "You'll never have grandchildren. You'll just have to watch your children grow old alone. Another futile boy without a purpose."

Tale picked at the edge of the table. She listened to the kitchen clock ticking, a cat crying somewhere outside. "I'm not having a boy," she said softly.

Kerise placed her hands on the table and leaned in. "What?"

"I'm having a girl."

"Seriously?"

Tale nodded.

"Then that, Tale, that should be more than enough to make you do this."

12

From her workstation, Minnie could look straight through two panes of glass to where Hector was sat, with his back to her, checking data. She knew what the data would say without even looking at it. They all did. It hadn't changed for almost three months. They were losing control, and they knew it. Even though no one was actually saying it.

Minnie also knew what Hector's report would say. They'd all written the same sentences over and over, trying to dress the truth up in scientific jargon, trying to turn all the negatives into something that sounded hopeful in part at least. But it wasn't fooling anyone anymore.

Minnie guessed that they were living on borrowed time with this project. That soon enough, it would be shut down and branded a failure. The staff would be redeployed, and— Minnie looked over at the Mother. The Daughters would probably survive, but she was more pipes than person these days. Even with Minnie's limited medical training, she knew there was no hope of getting her out of the system alive.

Minnie looked back towards Hector. They were meant to be having their date tomorrow night, and she'd spent the last two days thinking up excuses to cancel.

As if able to sense her eyes on him, he turned around. Minnie ducked behind her own screen while her cheeks flamed.

"Dammit," she muttered.

"What's that?" He was at her door.

Keeping her back to him to conceal her flushed cheeks, she replied as coolly as she could. "Just struggling to reword this report. It feels like I've used every possible permutation a million times already."

"You probably have."

"Yeah, there's only so many ways to say 'things are shit'."

She heard him shift his feet. She'd made him uncomfortable. Women weren't supposed to swear, especially in front of men. The blush returned, and she buried her chin into her chest.

The silence hung between them for a moment like a hideous gaping mouth, letting them dwell before swallowing them up.

They were both rescued by the booming voice of Jarrett as he descended the stairs to the Main.

"Listen up, people, we have had a request for volunteers." He stopped three stairs up and everyone gathered round slowly. No one was going to push their way to the front until they knew what they might be volunteering for.

"They're looking for anyone with medical training, so that's all of you. It seems that the project to offer healthcare to the slum women has been a little too successful, and they need some help to clear the backlog. I don't want to have to assign anyone who doesn't want to go, so please can we have some volunteers?"

"Do we get any extra benefits?" someone asked.

Jarrett chewed his lip. "I will see if I can negotiate something, but for now, the only benefit is a few days out of this place, and more choice of where to go for lunch."

"I'll go," someone else said, raising their hand. "Change of scenery," he added, obviously feeling the need to justify his decision. Nearly all of them had grown up on Newstone or Haverhead, and the thought of getting close to women from The Floor wasn't an attractive proposition.

"I guess I could go," said another voice. "It'll be nice to see daylight."

"I'll go too," said Minnie, shooting her hand into the air.

The people around her nodded and muttered to one another. She didn't have to offer up a justification; it was expected that any woman would want to help with women's problems. Slowly lowering her hand, she realised that she was shaking.

Jarrett was still asking for more volunteers, but his voice was drowned in the swell of blood through

Minnie's ears. She'd be on The Hope, working with slum women. It couldn't be more perfect.

Jarrett clapped his hands loudly and brought Minnie's attention back to the room.

"All right, thank you very much for volunteering, I did not fancy the job of assigning some of you lazy, reluctant bastards. And on a more positive note, that's the end of shift, so pack up your shit and get the hell out of here. Go and drink and be merry or whatever you get up to when you're not slaving around this place. Volunteers, I need you here bright and early at 7am. Do not be late, or I will come looking for you, and you do not want that to happen, believe me. Goodnight."

People began drifting towards the door, shrugging their white coats off their tired shoulders and onto the pegs. After what was termed as a 'triple shift', which was as equally gruelling as it sounded, no one was up for much merriment. Their beds were calling.

Minnie turned as someone gently touched her arm, and looked up into Hector's face.

"I guess I'll have to get used to not seeing you around for a few days then," he said.

"I guess."

Buffeted along by the crowd, they burst out of the Main into the corridor beyond.

"Look after the Mother for me, won't you?" Minnie said. "You know no one else cares."

He squeezed her hand. "You know I will. And I'm looking forward to tomorrow."

Minnie forced a smile. "Me too."

"So, are you headed back to your room? Or are you hungry at all?"

"Actually, I fancy a walk. It gets so stuffy down in the Main, I could do with some air."

"I know what you mean."

"Yeah, I'm just going to sit somewhere quiet," Minnie added hastily. "You know, gather my thoughts."

Hector nodded. He seemed to have got the hint. "Well, enjoy your time on The Hope. It's important work."

"Yes, it will be good to make a difference."

Hector stopped walking. They'd reached The Keep, the staff accommodation behind The Eye. This was where the women went one way, and the men went the other.

"Goodnight then," Minnie said.

Hector nodded. "Goodnight."

As Minnie turned away, someone nudged her hard from the other side, knocking her off balance.

"You two seem friendly," giggled Bianca, slipping her arm into Minnie's.

"Er... yeah." Minnie cursed to herself as she felt her face flush.

"So what's the story? I want all the gossip."

"There really isn't any."

"Don't lie. I saw you return home the other night with a dress box. You've got a date, haven't you?"

She nudged Minnie again with her pointy elbow.

Minnie grimaced. "Yeah, ok, we have a date

tomorrow."

"You see," Bianca screeched. "I knew there was something in it. I'm very intuitive."

Minnie smiled. "You should be careful saying things like that. You wouldn't want to end up in the Main, would you?"

Bianca closed her mouth tight. Minnie's smile broadened.

"I should get to my room, it's getting late."

"Bye, Bianca." Minnie turned onto her own corridor, and swiped her ID implant over the door's entrance pad. The door slid aside, and she stepped through.

Almost everything in her room was administration issued. The walls were bare, the furnishings functional and plain. Minnie looked up at the dress hanging on the outside of her wardrobe. It was the first fancy thing she'd ever owned. And it was the only beautiful thing in her room.

As an employee in The Eye, her accommodation and all of her meals were provided free. All she had to spend her wages on were frivolities, yet she'd never bought any before. She needed to change that. But she wasn't about to make this place homely. It was a prison, and it should feel like one.

Pulling open the drawer on her bedside table, she dug through for a notebook and pen. She needed to let Kerise know where she'd be.

It was cold outside, and Minnie was glad for the thick cardigan she'd thrown on. It had deep pockets, and the letter was buried inside one of them.

On the short walk across the lawn, she passed seven armed officers. Each of them stopped to greet her politely, and enquire as to where she was going so late at night. Had she been a man, they'd have likely ignored her.

"Just getting some air," she said to each of them. "Then I'm off to bed." It seemed to satisfy them all, but Minnie knew that any one of them could request to search her, for no reason, and that she would have to let them.

It wasn't uncommon for the female staff to be searched. The guards saw it as a bit of fun, and a way to get a quick grope of something they were unlikely to ever have legitimately. And, of course, a blind eye was turned. It was harmless, after all.

Minnie leaned against the tree Kerise had dropped out of when they first met. She had no idea if Kerise had ever been back here, but she couldn't leave The Head, and this was the only thing she could think of. She looked up into the branches. Would it catch in the leaves if she simply tossed it up? Would it blow back down with the first breeze that caught it? Probably. She couldn't risk it.

She looked around, counted to five, and then hauled herself up into the branches. She climbed up some way before she found the ideal place. A strong fork, the perfect sitting spot, and, at eye level, a hole in the bark.

Minnie rolled the letter and pushed one end of it in.

She looked up at The Eye. Sitting here gave her the perfect view of it. Kerise must have sat here. She ran her hand over the branch, and her finger caught on something. She leaned in closer, squinting in the darkness.

It was a heart, carved into the tree with a knife. And inside the heart was the letter M.

13

Minnie leaned back in her chair and sighed. She'd been working non-stop all morning; woman after woman after woman. No wonder they needed help down here. But after a lifetime of inadequate healthcare, the women from The Floor all had their little niggles. Things they'd lived with for years, and never had the opportunity, or the money, to have fixed.

She closed her eyes for a moment, and her head swam with exhaustion. How would she get through the rest of the day? The rest of the week? Thankfully, her and Hector had already agreed on an unfashionably early time for their dinner date due to their hectic work schedules.

Her mind just began to drift, taking her from awake to snoozing, when a commotion woke her. An argument.

She stood, opened the door to her treatment room, and peered out. Looking along the corridor, she wasn't the only curious one.

"Get back!" ordered the officer at the front door. "You can't get in without being registered."

"I need help! Look at me!"

"Not without an ID bracelet. Now get back!"

"You're meant to be helping us."

"Look, lady, I'm armed, and I am authorised to use force, so get back."

"Fine, shoot me. I'm not leaving."

Minnie strode up the corridor and placed her hand on the officer's arm.

"No one's shooting anyone," she said. Her heart was hammering, but she somehow managed to keep her voice steady. She looked up into Kerise's bloodied face, and breathed deeply. She couldn't let the officer see even a flash of recognition in her eyes. "I'll treat her."

"Strict instructions, only registered women can access the healthcare."

"Look at her, she needs medical assistance now. I'll patch her up, and then she's yours to deal with."

The officer hesitated. "But the rules—"

"I was dragged down here from The Head to give medical assistance to those who needed it. Are you going to prevent me from doing that? Am I going to have to inform my bosses that you were obstructive and prevented me from carrying out that task?"

The officer looked down at her, and she could see her own face reflected in his visor. He sighed.

"Fine, treat her. But bring her back to me when you're done."

"Thank you." Minnie turned to Kerise. "This way."

As Minnie clicked the door of her treatment room shut, her legs gave way, and she found herself on her knees. She felt Kerise's hands slip under her arms, lifting her, sitting her on the stretcher.

"Lay back," Kerise said. "You've had a shock." She eased Minnie's head down to the pillow, and smoothed back her hair. "That was really brave."

"I didn't feel brave."

"Well, you certainly fooled me." Kerise dragged over a chair and sat down.

Minnie took a deep, shaking breath. "I didn't fool myself." She looked at Kerise, and reached out to her. "Your face. We need to get you sorted."

"No, no, it's animal blood. From the butchers. I'm fine. But I knew I'd have to argue my way in here. They couldn't deny that I needed help looking like this."

"You got my letter then."

"I did. That was very clever of you." She grinned. "You're certainly my daughter."

Minnie's stomach flipped. It felt good to hear it, but scary too. She'd been alone for so long, and, alone, she'd had nothing to lose. But here she was, doing the most dangerous things she'd ever done, and suddenly, she had everything to lose.

"So," Kerise said, "tell me everything."

Minnie took a deep breath.

"I don't know where to start."

"Start anywhere. We'll fill in as we go."

"Ok. I work in a place called the Main. It's a place where all the pipes come together, pipes that feed the water supply to the whole of Falside. Well, barring The Floor, of course. Which is lucky for them. For years, the administration have been experimenting, adding things to the water, spreading it out to the population. Sometimes it's good things; vitamins, vaccines. Sometimes it's tranquillisers. Then they found that they could control other things too. You wouldn't believe how advanced things have become.

"They discovered that they could control fertility and birth rates, putting them in direct control of the population. And then they found a way to influence the genders of the babies born. They could control the amount of X chromosomes present in sperm. They could slow down the production of girls. Make them rare. Make them special."

"And put them in danger," suggested Kerise.

"Exactly. The women had no choice but to come to the administration and beg for protection. And once the administration controlled the women, they controlled everything. They controlled the birth rate, and they controlled the men. But it wasn't enough, and it wasn't perfect. Whatever they put into the water supply, people seemed to become immune to it, and quickly too. They had to keep tweaking the recipe. It meant more research, more money, and periods when they had no control at all.

"They were also researching psychics. Learning how to control them. I'm sure you know that water seems to improve psychic connectivity.

Its reach. And they wondered if they could use psychics instead. And they could. They plumbed them straight in."

"What do you mean?"

"I mean they're part of the pipe system. Pipes go into their bodies, and out of their bodies. Their psychic powers run all over the city, into every single home. They can hear everything, see everything, influence everything."

Kerise rubbed her forehead, smearing blood across it. "They're plumbed straight in," she repeated quietly. "And they can control people through their drinking water?"

Minnie nodded. "They can plant thoughts, intentions, and the administration controls them. They're not considered people anymore. Their names have been erased from the data. They're nothing but company assets. Like me."

Kerise reached out and squeezed her hand. "Can they be saved?"

"There are nine women being used. Eight Daughters, and the Mother. She controls it all, drawing on the power of the Daughters. The Mother..." Minnie shook her head. "There's no way that she could be unplumbed. The Daughters, however, could survive. If they had immediate medical attention. But the Main isn't equipped for it. Because there's no intention to ever un-plumb them. They'd have to be removed and quickly taken to a hospital. Any delay would reduce their chances significantly.

"The psychics have worked far better than the

synthetic additives. Plus, they came with an unexpected bonus; they reported back."

"What do you mean?"

"They read the minds of the people, and reported back to the administration. Mostly it's babble, snippets, unintelligible. But now and again, they would shout out something helpful. Something the administration could use. People hated being spied on through their technology, but at least, back then, they actually knew they were being spied on. This is something different altogether. Thoughts that they've barely even thought. Fleeting impulses that they'd never actually act on. How many times have you considered doing something terrible, and dismissed it just as quickly?

"But the Mother knew what was happening. The Daughters are little more than batteries, barely conscious, but the Mother is so strong. She's fiery, and difficult to control. She started misinforming, purposefully. Sending the administration out on wild goose chases. She was laughing at them."

Minnie looked up at Kerise and they grinned at one another.

"As a result, they tranquillise her now. Not that that even works particularly well. Like I said, she's too strong. Unruly. Taking matters into her own hands. The crisis with the female birth rate, that's all her. The administration withdrew that strategy years ago. The city's buckling, and it can't continue for much longer the way things are. She's doing this herself, she's bringing Falside to its knees."

"Why?"

"I think she's protecting women. Stopping more of them being born to simply become part of the regime. And she's trying to break it too. Bring down the administration from the inside."

Minnie found herself grinning again.

"Why don't they just abandon the project altogether?"

Minnie shrugged. "Lots of reasons. They've poured a lot of money into it. Man hours too. Plus, they have nothing to replace it with. They stopped researching and creating additives years ago, that technology has completely stalled. Plus, the information they get back is invaluable. Sure, it's interspersed with false reports, but they've got the Mother hooked up to brain monitoring now, and they can tell the difference between the genuine reports and the ones she makes up. Well, mostly. It looks like she's learning to fake that too."

"Sounds like she'd be good as part of the resistance."

"I think she already is." Minnie swung her legs over the side of the stretcher and sat up, facing Kerise. She reached out and took her hands in hers. "And I am too. I want you to know that." She smiled. "I guess it was in my blood. I hope this is useful to you."

"It is. And your support is… well, we could never have even dreamt of having someone in The Eye." Kerise looked down at their linked hands. "It means everything to me that you're with us. I would have hated it if they'd completely brainwashed you."

"They tried."

"As long as you stay safe. Take whatever precautions you need. I can't lose you again."

"You won't. And when all this is over, there'll be no one to stand in the way of us being together."

Kerise rubbed her face, but through the blood, Minnie couldn't tell if she was crying.

"So, you don't know the names of any of the women they're using?"

"No, I do. I know them all. I dug through the archives. I whisper their names into their ears. I don't want them to forget who they really are."

"The Mother. She's called Selene Richards, right?"

"Yes. How did you know?"

"I know her daughter." Kerise thought for a moment. "Can they hear you when you speak to them? Are they conscious?"

"I like to think the Daughters can hear me, but they never react. The Mother, however, she reacts to everything we say. She's fully aware."

"Can you give her a message?"

Minnie nodded.

"Can you tell her that her daughter's coming for her? That Maeve is coming to get her."

"I will."

Kerise stood up. "Is there another way out of here? I don't think I should try the front again."

"Yes, there's a delivery entrance at the back. It's meant to be locked, but the men go out there to smoke, so it never is."

Kerise bent and hugged Minnie tight, pressing

a kiss into her hair. "Thank you so much for this. And I'll see you soon."

Minnie nodded. Her throat was too swollen with tears to speak.

Kerise nodded and stepped out of the room.

Minnie exhaled and leaned against the edge of the stretcher. She looked at her trolley of instruments, the stainless steel reflecting her flushed face. Grabbing the edge of it, she threw it sideways, toppling its contents to the floor. Jumping up, she slammed the door shut, pulled it open again, and stuck her head out into the corridor.

"Help!" she shouted. "Can I have some help here?"

The officer lurched towards her, his hand hovering over his holster.

"She attacked me!" Minnie gestured towards the back door. "She went that way."

"Are you alright?" he asked her.

"I'm fine."

He lumbered down the corridor towards the back door. "Probably long gone by now," he muttered.

"Hopefully," Minnie whispered to herself.

14

Tale braced her hands against the edge of the worktop and stared at the kettle's exhale of steam. It was a lot to absorb. They'd always suspected that the administration was somehow controlling the birth rate of girls, but she couldn't have possibly imagined the truth of it.

"You have to stop coming here, Kerise," she said. "I don't want Colby seeing you."

"Yeah, you wouldn't want him to know who you really are, would you?"

"Who I *was*. I'm someone else now."

"Who?"

Tale turned round and looked at Kerise who was leaning across the table towards her.

"I'm a wife. And a mother."

"You're a drone."

"I'm doing what I have to."

"You're conforming. You're giving up." Kerise shook her head slowly. "If Freda could see you now."

Tale turned back around, her throat tight with

tears. She blinked them back. "I know. I know what's at stake. I know how important this is. But you need to understand how important it is for me to keep my family safe. I have so much to lose now."

"We all do."

Tale turned back to Kerise. "You have your daughter now. So you have to appreciate my need to protect mine."

"And what about making a better future for her? For her daughters? For those women plumbed in up at The Eye?"

"I'm sorry about them, I am, but this simply isn't my battle anymore."

"How can you say that? You're a woman. You're carrying your little girl. I just—" She threw her arms into the air. "I just don't understand you."

"I cannot risk getting killed, Kerise." Tale slammed her hand down on the worktop behind her. "Do you understand that?"

Kerise closed her mouth and slid her hands into her lap. She nodded slowly.

"When they took Minnie away they took away everything I had. I wanted to die. For such a long time, I wanted to. And then, I simply didn't care whether I did or not. I threw myself into every dangerous situation I could. I joined the resistance. I took every illegal job I could find. I never said no to anything. I had no limits, because I had nothing to lose but my life. And what worth was that? But now..." She nodded again. "Yes, I do understand. But I'm not asking you to storm The Eye with me. I just want you to write one more issue of Asteria. I'm not asking that much."

"It still risks my life, you know that. And Colby's. And..." Her hand ran instinctively over her stomach.

"She's the very reason that there's no risk. They're not going to kill you. They wouldn't dare."

"Perhaps not yet, but they could take away everything I love. Like they did to you."

"In sixteen years' time, they will anyway."

Tale thought for a moment, her brow furrowed. Could she risk sixteen years for the possibility of forever? Of freeing her daughter completely? Of freeing herself?

That is, if she wanted to be freed.

The thought surprised her. It had crept up on her like a shiver, like a shadow. And then it lingered. At the very least, she could fight to have the choice.

She nodded, hard. "I'll do it. One more time. The last hurrah."

Kerise leapt from her chair and took Tale's hands in hers. "It's going to be the start of everything."

15

Kerise held Tale by the shoulders at arms length and considered her.

"Thank you, so much," she said. "I really do appreciate it. I know what you're risking."

Tale shrugged. "The greater good, and all that."

Kerise leant forward and kissed Tale's cheek. "And it will be so, so good. I promise. The world will never be the same again after this."

The front door clicked and opened. Tale glanced over her shoulder and pushed Kerise towards the back door.

"You have to go, that'll be Colby."

"See you soon," Kerise said as she slipped out into the garden.

"Who's that?" Colby was leaning on the worktop, peering out of the window.

Tale jumped. "No one."

He looked at her, one eyebrow arched.

"I mean, just an old friend."

"Just an old friend? As in someone from the

resistance?"

Tale looked at the floor. "She just came to say hello," she muttered.

He stepped towards her. "I don't want you to associate with those people anymore."

"I'm sorry, I—"

"I was warned about you," he said, cutting her off. "My friends said I was crazy to choose you. Everyone knew what you were, what you did. My parents hated the idea, you know that. But I took you anyway, because I thought you'd put all of that silliness behind you."

"You took me anyway? Am I supposed to be eternally grateful?"

"I didn't mean it like that."

"What did you mean, Colby? Do you see yourself as some sort of hero? Because you took on 'damaged goods'?" She gestured the quotation marks in the air.

"I don't see myself as—"

"Because you're such a great guy, aren't you? You pretend that you stand for equality, but you're enjoying the establishment just as much as the next guy. You like owning me. You like telling me who I can and can't be friends with, what I can and can't be."

"You know I'm not like that."

"You pretend not to be. You say all the right things, but deep down you're still a man, and you're the same as all the others."

He grabbed her wrist. "Stop it!"

"Or what? You'll hit me?"

He let go of her and stepped back. "No."

Tale could hear the shock and hurt in his voice, see it plastered over his face, but she continued anyway.

"You said it yourself; the resistance is nothing but 'silliness'. Equality is nothing but 'silliness'. Freedom is nothing but 'silliness'. It's easy to see our efforts as ridiculous when you're already enjoying your freedom. It's easy to ridicule those that you oppress to oppress us further."

"I do not oppress you."

"You just told me that I can't be friends with those people anymore."

"I am trying to protect you."

"I don't need protecting! And certainly not from them." She jabbed a finger at him.

He nodded and took another step backwards. "I see. You need protecting from me, is that it? You say I'm just like other men, that we're all the same, so fine. If that's all you ever expected from me, then that's what I'll be."

He stepped forward again and cradled her chin in his hands, tilting her face up towards him.

"You will *not* see those people again. They are not allowed in *my* house. You will put all of those stupid thoughts out of your head. And if you defy me, you will be sorry. There. Is that what you want? There, I did it. Now I am the monster you obviously see me as." He dropped his hands. "Do *not* defy me, Tale, or so help you."

Tale swallowed hard. The tears pricked at the back of her eyes, but she did not want him to see her cry.

"I hate you," she whispered.

"Well, fuck you," he replied, his voice cold and flat. He turned sharply and marched out of the room.

Tale jumped as the front door slammed shut. And then the tears came. Convulsing up from her stomach and flowing over her cheeks to drip from her chin. She bent forward, her hand gripping the edge of the worktop, her lungs heaving.

She grabbed onto the pain that overwhelmed her, that almost brought her to her knees. She gripped it and inspected it, turned it over and around. It was so horribly familiar that she had no need to ask its name. Its name was betrayal.

Squeezing it, Tale formed it into a hard rock, and settled it into her heart. It fitted perfectly, cradled into the muscle, and somehow made Tale feel more complete. She'd carried that stone for years after Freda left, and now it had returned to her. The familiar heaviness of it was almost comforting. It was what she deserved.

Colby had let her see a different life, just a glimpse, let her wallow for a moment, sink into it, feel its warmth on her skin. He had teased her with it, and then torn it from her. She knew now that things would never be different.

Unless she made them different.

She looked up as she heard the front door open. Colby's footsteps came quickly down the hall, his arms closed around her, lifted her, and his face nuzzled into her hair.

"I'm so sorry," he whispered. "I'm so sorry. I don't want to tell you what to do, but I'm just so scared. I'm scared I might lose you, and our baby. I couldn't live without you, Tale, it would kill me. I love you so much, I love you."

"That's the first time you've ever said that," Tale whispered back.

"Is that ok?"

Tale nodded. "Yes. I like it."

Even as that small stone in her heart crumbled into dust, her heart filled with another feeling. She remembered this one too, but she hadn't felt it in a long time.

16

Hector stood up as Minnie approached the table. He smiled and opened his hands towards her.

"You look absolutely—" he stopped and looked down at her feet. "You're hilarious."

Looking down, Minnie saw the scuffed steel toecaps of her work boots sticking out from under the folds of her skirt. "I feel so preened and primped, and... I just needed something that made me feel like me under all of this."

"I get that," he said, gesturing to himself. His usually unkempt hair was smoothed down, his jawline cleanly shaven, his suit crisp and smart. "But I figured we ought to blend in. Didn't want to seem suspicious." He winked.

They'd decided to have their date in The Eye; which saved Minnie asking for another pass. Other than the staff canteen, which was built purely for function, there was The Rosehip. It was a sumptuous, expensive restaurant mostly used only by those on the higher pay grades. Minnie had insisted on contributing to the cost, despite Hector's protestations.

Minnie glanced around as she sat down and smoothed out her skirt. Everyone was dressed up; suits, bow-ties, evening and cocktail dresses. She wondered what it must be like to live like this; for such finery to be an everyday experience.

She smiled at Hector over the top of her menu. She'd imagined the date would be excruciating with them struggling to relate outside of work, but by the time their starters had arrived, any initial tension had fallen away as they chatted easily.

"We shouldn't talk shop," Hector said suddenly. "I want to know what Minnie's like outside of the office."

Minnie stared at her food. "There's really not much to tell. When I'm not working, I'm sitting in my room."

"There must be something you like to do."

"I like to walk around the gardens. Look down at the city."

The city I'm not allowed to enter without written permission, she thought.

"What about you?" she asked.

"I like to play snooker. And I like going to the cinema." He cleared his throat.

Minnie guessed the source of his embarrassment. Women weren't allowed to the cinema unaccompanied, supposedly for their own safety.

"It's ok," she said. "I haven't seen a movie in years, not since I was a kid. They used to let me watch them sometimes."

"It must've been hard, growing up, not knowing where you came from." He shrugged. "Still not knowing."

Minnie smiled tightly. "I guess when you don't know any different, it just seems kind of normal."

They both looked up as the waiter collected their empty dishes and brought their mains.

"This is really good," Hector said, prodding the chicken with his fork.

"Mine too," Minnie replied quickly, her fork already halfway to her mouth.

She ate hungrily, and couldn't help but wonder what Kerise was eating tonight. Or where she was eating. She realised that she knew nothing about her; all they'd ever talked about was their plans for revolution. She'd not used that word for it before, but that's what it was. It was a heavy word, and a heavy secret to carry. It made it all seem suddenly real.

She blinked and looked up, only then realising Hector had been speaking to her.

"Am I boring you?" he asked.

She shook her head. "No, I'm sorry. I just have things on my mind."

"Like what?"

She shook her head again. "Nothing really."

"It's clearly keeping you preoccupied."

She looked hard at him, studied his eyes, chewed her lip, thought for a minute. She'd never really trusted anyone before, until she'd met Kerise. Maybe it was the excitement of finally having someone else that she could rely on and confide in, that made her want more of it. Maybe it was just the wine. But she truly believed she could trust him.

"I found my mother," Minnie said, leaning forward. She watched Hector's reaction closely.

He glanced around him before answering. "What do you mean?"

"Well, strictly speaking, she found me."

"You're a ward. You're not meant to even *have* parents. And you're certainly not meant to go looking for them."

"I didn't. Like I said, she found me."

Hector exhaled sharply. "This is big, Minnie. You could get into a lot of trouble over this."

"I can trust you though, can't I?"

"Of course, of course." He reached forward and their fingers touched on the table. "I just don't want you putting yourself in danger."

Minnie looked down at their hands and slowly withdrew hers into her lap.

"There's more, isn't there?" said Hector.

"You and I both know the administration is on the verge of collapse, that all of this is buckling. We're just going to help it on its way."

"Are you crazy?"

"We're just giving it a little push."

"You realise what you're saying? This is treason."

Minnie glared at the edge of the table. She hadn't thought of it like that before. Kerise made it sound like their only option, like the right thing to do. They were taking away the bad, weren't they?

"You have the luxury of living freely, Hector. Imagine how it is for me. I need to have you on my side."

Hector leaned back and ran his hands through his hair, returning it to its usual untidiness. He leaned forward again.

"Only to make sure you don't end up getting yourself killed."

17

Maeve lay her hands flat on the table. She stared at her hot coffee between them. She watched the fine strings of steam tangle around one another, somehow always managing to unfurl before fading into nothing.

She turned and looked at Faith, playing on the bed.

"So what exactly do you want me to do?" she asked, looking back at Kerise.

"Just distribute some magazines, that's all. Hand them out, leave them in places people can find them."

"That sounds simple enough. What are they about?"

Kerise looked at her intensely. "The truth."

Maeve suppressed a giggle. "The truth?"

Kerise nodded. "The people need to know."

"The people need to know," Maeve echoed again. "And what exactly do the people need to know? This better not be some revolutionary thing I'm going to get arrested for. I have Faith, I can't get into any kind of trouble."

Kerise threw her hands in the air. "What is it with everyone wanting to protect their children all of a sudden?"

"It's kind of a parenting thing. As you well know."

"Well, this is going to protect your daughter. And mine. And every daughter ever born."

Maeve sighed. "So, it is revolutionary stuff."

"How can the truth be revolutionary?"

Maeve laughed. "Don't try to bluff me, Kerise, you know better than anyone: the truth is always revolutionary."

"Ok, so it's revolutionary. But people need to know this. *You* need to know this."

"Why me in particular?"

Kerise reached a hand across the table, but stopped short of making contact.

"Because it's about the psychics that the administration took."

A weight dropped through the bottom of Tale's stomach, turning her insides into a void.

"My mother?"

Kerise shook her head slightly. "I don't know. Minnie doesn't know any of their names. They're considered assets, not people, and their names have been erased from any paperwork. But maybe, maybe your mother is there."

"What are they doing with them?"

"They're using them to control the population, through the drinking water. The psychics are quite literally plumbed in."

Maeve covered her mouth with her hand. For a moment, she could feel the rush of water, flowing out of her body, pouring through the city, flooding into other bodies, other minds. She could feel the clamour of voices, the torrent of a thousand thoughts travelling with the current. She gripped hold of the edge of the table to stop herself from drowning.

"Are you alright?" Kerise asked.

Maeve opened her mouth, but her throat was full of foam. She nodded and gestured for Kerise to continue.

"The administration are using them to spy on everyone. Everyone from The Hope upwards, at least. And we were right; the administration were controlling the birthrate of girls."

"Were?" spluttered Maeve.

"Originally, they were using synthetic additives in the water, but they didn't work that well. That's when they switched to using the psychics. But, Maeve, the psychics are fighting back. What's happening now is not the administration's doing. The psychics have gone rogue, cutting girls being born to almost nothing. They're bringing everything down. The city can't cope with so few women anymore. Everything's about to break. And the administration is going to break with it. The psychics, they're a part of the resistance."

Maeve swallowed hard, her throat burning. "What are we going to do?"

"First, we let the public know the truth."

"They'll never believe it."

"You'd be surprised what desperate people will believe. The administration will do everything they can to discredit us, but once that seed of doubt is planted, it will root in far quicker than they can dig it out. That's why we need to distribute everywhere, and quickly."

"Can we save them?"

Kerise nodded. "We're sure as hell going to try."

Maeve looked over at Faith. "She's going to meet her grandmother."

Kerise's hand made contact then, gripping hold of Maeve's fingers.

18

Tale looked up at the front doors of The Paper Duchess. Here she was again. But this time, it didn't feel familiar, like coming home. This time it felt like she was walking to the gallows.

She lifted a heavy foot and planted it on the first step. The door above her flew open and Denver stepped out, waving his arms at her.

"No, no, no!" he shouted. "Don't come this way. I've done something special for you at the back. Not this way."

It took Tale a moment to understand what he was saying, her mind was too full of dark premonitions. She shook her head clear and nodded.

The small window at the back of the building had been knocked through, though Tale wondered how Denver could have managed to wield a sledgehammer. He was thinner every time she saw him. The makeshift doorway had two steps leading up to it, and another two to match on the inside. Denver had left the whole building open to anyone.

Tale ducked through the crumbling opening and into the room beyond. The space had been emptied, and as she crossed to the door, she heard a key turn in the lock.

"I'm glad you've had the sense to lock that," she said, as she pulled the door open.

"I know it's risky," Denver replied, "but I cannot have you going through the front and registering your ID implant again."

"Has something happened?"

He cocked his head. "Come and look."

She followed his gangly gait up the corridor and into the main room. She looked around, mouth open.

The shelves had been ransacked; books strewn across the floor, some bookcases had been toppled. But it was the lack of books that was most obvious. The shelves that still held some bore gaping holes in their collections. The books strewn across the floor were meagre in number. Denver's life work. Pulled apart.

Tale looked at him. His jaw was hard. Set. But it was the look in his eyes that really scared her. They weren't hurt, or defeated. They were ablaze with determination.

"What happened?" Tale ventured.

"You happened." He shook his head. "No, I'm sorry, that's not fair. This happened." He gestured to the air around them. "All of this. This city, this world, this..."

Tale didn't know the words either. She stepped forward and placed a hand on his arm. It was rigid, unyielding.

He took a deep breath. "Two days after you'd been here, and logged your entrance." He flung his hand towards the front door. "They came. About ten officers. 'Reminded' me of the rules regarding selling books to women, married or not. And then they 'confiscated' whatever they didn't like the look of. Don't worry, the cookery and home economics shelves are still intact. Couldn't risk a woman getting ideas from anything else though. Something revolutionary like fiction. Stories of a world where everything isn't totally shit."

"I'm so sorry, Denver."

He shook his head slowly. "It's not your fault, they were just waiting for an excuse. It's just all those words that will never be read now. All that knowledge, understanding. The enlightenment."

"If we get out the other end of this alive, we can write new books. People will want to hear our story. And we can't let them hide the truth."

Denver cleared his throat and turned away from the shelves. "Well, it's the women's turn this time. You can write your stories."

"That's what Kerise sent me here to do."

"Your office is all ready for you, just how you left it."

She squeezed his arm. "Things are going to get better."

He looked away. "Go. Go write your inflammatory magazine."

Tale worked furiously, her fingers flying over the keyboard. When her pregnancy made her uncomfortable, she walked the corridor for a while, pacing up and down. It helped to clear her head too; focussing and organising the words.

When she had finished, she printed off a single copy, and took it through to Denver. She placed it on the bar and heaved herself up onto a stool.

Denver turned the sheet of paper around to face him.

"So this is it? This single sheet of paper is the end of the administration."

"I certainly hope so. Can you imagine?" She giggled; the sound escaping in bursts.

"You know, I actually can't. What comes after all of this?"

Tale shrugged. "I guess we'll just have to wait and find out." She flashed a smile at him. "Exciting, eh?"

"Every now and again I see a shred of Freda in you. More so since she left."

Tale pressed her lips together and nodded once.

"Sorry," Denver said. "It still hurts, huh?"

Tale shrugged. "Only when I think about it."

He waggled a finger at her. "You should deal with those unresolved issues, Tale, before they come back and bite you on the ass."

"Nothing's biting me on the ass."

Denver slapped the counter. "Back to business. How many copies of this are we going to need?"

Tale smiled. "A lot. A hell of a lot."

19

Kerise looked up. The pile of papers were tossed from the balcony above her, fluttering down like autumn leaves. They fell lightly, caught on the breeze, they carouselled, spiralled, pirouetted. They danced in the air, hands clasped together, spinning one another, lifting one another, locked in a ritual of seduction.

But they didn't seduce the people below. The spell broke as the papers landed. As they touched hands, as they touched the ground, their magic faded, and the words became heavy and leaden.

The eyes that roved them dulled in confusion, darkened in anger. They looked to others, looking for validation, for confirmation. Some tossed them aside, disbelieving, but the seeds were sown. And the doubt spread like weeds.

It rooted itself in dissatisfaction, leafed in frustration, and flowered in hatred.

20

"Where are your shoes?" Maeve cried. "Come on, we're going to miss everything."

The spring festival was Maeve's favourite event of the year, and she found herself excited and impatient to take Faith for the first time.

She had vague memories of being there with her mother; eating toffee apples, and sweet doughnuts dipped in honey. She remembered stroking an owl, watching a man pull money from his nostrils, and gazing up at stilt walkers passing by far above her. She remembered her hand held tightly in her mother's as they pushed their way through the crowded streets. She remembered the sound of her mother laughing, and how they danced until long after sunset.

She looked at Faith. No matter what happened, she wanted her to have those happy memories too.

She knelt and buckled Faith's shoes, tugged a jacket onto her arms, and dragged her from the house.

The festival events were mostly concentrated along The Wall, but spilled down every side street with people setting up stalls in their own doorways, or tempting people inside with promises of entertainment 'the likes of which they've never seen before'. Of course, they'd seen it all before, it was the same every year, but it didn't matter. The atmosphere made everything seem magical and unique.

The streets were already tightly packed with people, and not just residents of The Floor. Citizens from the upper levels of Falside poured down the narrow steps to sample the delights of the spring festival.

"Hello, Maeve!"

Maeve jumped and turned around. She smiled broadly and accepted the tight embrace offered to her.

"Madam Lemaire," Maeve said, disappearing into layers of lace and velvet. "It's so good to see you."

"You're looking well." She bent down to Faith. "And this can't be little Faith. She's grown so big."

"She's four now."

Madam Lemaire gasped. "Four. My goodness." She straightened up. "Well, you certainly look like you've done right by her. You really seem to have landed on your feet. I'm glad, you deserved some happiness."

"Thank you. So, how's business?"

"Good, always good. We'll never run out of

customers. Just drumming up some business for tonight. Spring festival is always busy once the sun goes down."

Maeve giggled. "I'm sure it is."

"Especially with all the visitors. Lots of frustrated men with money to burn."

Madam Lemaire stepped closer to Maeve and took hold of her wrist, wrapping her hand around the ID bracelet.

"You're the sort of person who might do well to know this. There's someone who can deactivate these; let you move around freely without being tracked. If you need it, come and see me. Of course, that sort of thing doesn't come cheap, but I can help you out. Alright?"

Maeve nodded. "That is useful to know. I may well take you up on that offer someday."

"Anytime. And if there's anything else you ever need, just come and ask."

"Actually..." Maeve dug into her bag and pulled out a pile of papers. "Can you give these to your girls, your customers? Anyone who comes through the door."

Madam Lemaire looked down at the copies of Asteria. She nodded. "One of my girls brought this back yesterday. If this is even halfway true, then yes, I'm happy to help." She ruffled Faith's hair. "You know there's always a safe place for this one down at The Slip. We're very good at hiding things. When all of this—" she waved the papers "blows up, we can keep her safe while you do what you need to do."

"That means a lot. Thank you."

Madam Lemaire hugged her again. "Stay safe," she whispered in her ear. And then, with a wave, she was swept away into the crowd.

Maeve bent down to Faith, brushing back her hair. As she straightened, her nose caught a scent. She breathed it in, closing her eyes.

"Doughnuts," she whispered. "Come on."

She fought her way through the crowd, deftly skipping along the wooden walkways. It hadn't rained in days, and the mud was dried hard into deep ruts. One false step could result in a twisted ankle. Or a broken one.

Maeve stopped at the doughnut cart and pulled out a credit. She waved it at the man. "One bag please."

The man smiled out from under a wide-brimmed hat. "Someone's keen."

Maeve blushed and shrugged. "They're my favourite."

He laughed, deep and gravelly, and his thick stomach pumped up and down. "Mine too," he replied with a wink.

As he lifted the small doughnuts from their tray, a snowstorm of sugar fell from them. He dropped them into a plastic bag, and reached for the honey. Holding the bottle high, he made a show of drizzling the golden liquid in. He gave the bag a quick shake and handed it over.

He glanced at Faith. "Don't eat them all at once. Wouldn't want to spoil your appetite."

Maeve giggled. "Oh, these won't even last five

minutes."

The man waved as they moved back into the flow of people, calling "they rarely do" after them.

The doughnuts succumbed to the squeeze of her fingers, the soft dough collapsing inwards, the warm honey coating her skin. She pulled one out, let it drip for a moment, and handed it to Faith.

"Careful, don't drop it."

Faith pushed it into her mouth, covering her lips with sugar and honey. She chewed with her mouth wide open in a grin and her eyes shut.

Maeve followed suit, filling her mouth with the warm cushion of sweetness, closing her eyes to bask in the indulgent sticky taste. For a moment, nothing else existed. The sounds around her faded, even the board beneath her feet became soft and mallow. She breathed in deeply, and in amongst the smell of hot food, animals, tobacco, beer, vomit, and the constant stench of the river, Maeve found the scent of her mother. A fragrance pulled through time, drawn across years, remembered and recreated in exquisite perfection. It trailed into her lungs where it balled itself into a sob, before being hurled back out into the world as Maeve choked it up. The tears on her cheeks brought her back to the present, and as she rubbed them away, she looked down at her own daughter. The tears came quickly, each one a droplet of agonising, raging love; too big an emotion to contain inside one body.

Faith knotted her hand into Maeve's skirt. "What's wrong Mummy? Why are you crying?"

Maeve lifted the girl onto her hip, and hugged

her tightly.

"They're happy tears," she whispered. "Mummy's just so happy to be here with you."

Maeve rubbed her face with her sleeve and slid Faith back to the floor, keeping a firm grip on her hand.

"Come on, let's go and see what's happening up along The Wall. But stay close, and don't let go of my hand. It's so busy, it would be easy to get pulled away in the crowd."

Faith nodded. "Ok, Mummy."

Above their heads, The Wall was strung with bunting that pitched back and forth across the street. Either side was lined with tents and stalls with bright awnings that flickered in the breeze like candlelight. The crowd pressed in tightly around them, and Maeve pulled Faith close against her as they pushed their way through.

Faith was captivated by the man with a monkey, laughing as the small creature ran up and down his arms. She was fascinated by a crystal stall, the clear gems casting rainbows that danced across her face. She stared, open mouthed, at the array of faces on a stall of puppets, she gazed at stunning hand-crafted candles, smoothed her hand along bowls carved from driftwood, sucked eagerly on another honeyed doughnut, and laughed loudly at a clown who tumbled and tripped in a hilarious performance of failed acrobatics.

All around them was sound and smell and colourful movement, and every moment of it was sugared with joy and excitement. Maeve's heart was fuller than she could ever remember it being before.

As they pushed their way up the street, the vendors called to them from other side; promising that their wares, or their performance would be the best they'd see all day.

"The land is pregnant now; its belly will become full and round, and so will yours!" cried a man waving skewers of dripping meat above his head.

"Catch the heart of the one you desire, or cover your rival's face with warts!" called a woman in a headscarf.

Faith tugged on Maeve's hand, pointing to a tent up ahead.

"Be amazed, be enthralled, be mystified as I draw magic from the ancient worlds!" the man shouted. He was bent almost double with age, his gnarled hand gripping the handle of an equally knotted staff. He turned towards them, one eye glistening in the sunlight, the other vanished behind fleshy, wrinkled waves of skin.

Maeve gasped, but Faith's grip on her hand tightened as she pulled forward.

"You want to watch the magic show?" Maeve asked.

"I do, I do!" She pulled forward again, and Maeve relented.

The man beckoned towards them, and flashes of light jumped from his fingers.

"Come, come," he said, "See what I have for you today." He clapped his hands, and white butterflies lifted from his palms like confetti. He held one of his hands out towards Maeve who placed a credit it in. The man scrumpled it into his fist, and as he opened his fingers again, the paper had transformed into a tiny white squirrel. It jumped from his hand, dispersing into mist before hitting the ground.

Faith squealed and clapped, Maeve stared at the fading wisps of smoke, dumbfounded.

"You see," the man said, "real magic still exists in the world. No matter what, there is always a miracle to be found. Or, if you cannot find one, you can always create one."

He turned his hands about and opened them to reveal a tiny white elephant on his palm. It walked around on his leathered skin, fanning its ears, raising its trunk into the air. He clapped his hands together, and the elephant was gone.

He looked up at Maeve and grinned with crooked, blackened teeth.

"It can be hard to believe, even when our eyes tell us the truth. But you should trust in yourself, because anything is possible."

Reaching up, he plucked something invisible from the air above his head. He balled it between his hands, moving it back and forth. His arms drooped as if it had become heavier.

"Things that were lost can still be found. Things that were broken..." He pressed his palms tightly together, and when he opened them again, a mug was sat on his palm. It had a pink flower on the side. He held it out to Maeve. "They can be mended."

Maeve slowly reached out and touched it. She felt it, solid, at the tips of her fingers.

"Take it," he said. "It's real."

Slipping her fingers into the handle, she lifted it from his hand. She could feel the weight of it, but it couldn't be real.

"This was broken," Maeve said. "In the riots. It was broken. I threw the pieces away."

She turned it over in her hands, inspecting it.

"Trust in yourself," the man said again. "You will be tried, and you will be tested, but if you only believe, you cannot fail." He grabbed her hands, pressing the mug between them. "Dark times will come, darker than you've ever known, but after the darkness comes light, and you must always believe in the rising of the sun. Believe that the dawn will come, no matter how long and empty the night may seem. You, Maeve, the dawn will ride with you, but there are sacrifices to be made. Not everyone can wake. Not everyone can stay. You can't keep hold of everything that you have. Are you ready?"

He released her from his grip and the mug was gone. Maeve could still feel the ghost of it, pressing into her palms. She stepped back.

"Come on, Faith," she said, reaching out for the girl's hand. It didn't come.

She turned and looked at the empty space Faith had been stood in.

"Faith?" She turned, her eyes flicking back and forth across the moving forest of legs. "Faith!" she yelled.

She spun around. "Faith!"

Maeve's heart fell from her body, leaving it empty and cold. The numbness crept over her skin, from head to toe, disconnecting her from every sense. She no longer heard the crowd, the music, the calls of the street sellers. She no longer smelt hot food, fresh fish, incense, leather. She no longer felt the ground beneath her feet, or the sun on her skin. Her mouth tasted only ash, and the colours faded to grey.

She couldn't even hear herself screaming Faith's name.

21

Faith pulled back, twisting around, reaching out. "Mummy," she whimpered.

"Sssh, sssh, it's ok, sweetheart, your Mummy asked me to take you for a little while. We're going to have some fun, alright?"

Faith relaxed a little, and followed along.

"Be careful up the steps, some of these are very steep and uneven, and it's busy here today. We're going up to The Hope. This is where you came from, but you won't remember." She bent and tucked a stray curl behind Faith's ear. "We're going to take you back where you belong."

Faith whimpered again, and glanced down the steps behind them.

"You do remember me though, don't you?"

Faith looked up at her, her face lightening. "Yes. You're Corinn."

22

Minnie flicked her head round as another scream echoed through the room. A group of officers clung tightly to the Mother's limbs, while her torso billowed back and forth like a ship's sail. Her head rolled back, her mouth opened, and another scream tore through the Main, followed by incoherent babble.

Minnie pushed back her chair and crossed to the door of her office.

"Stand back!" she cried out to them. "Give her room, you're crowding her!"

An officer lifted his hands into a shrug. "Then give her a shot. What else are we supposed to do?"

Minnie growled and ducked back inside. She pulled open a drawer and picked out a tranquilliser. She grabbed a pistol from the rack, and marched over to where the Mother was still fighting.

"Get back," Minnie ordered. "All of you." She knelt and smoothed back the Mother's hair. "It's alright, sssh, calm down."

As her efforts waned and she became still and

quiet, the officers retreated back to their posts by the door.

"It's just another bad dream," Minnie said soothingly. "But I've got a good dream for you, Selene. I need you to listen to me. I know that you can hear me."

Minnie glanced over her shoulder, but the officers were already lounging around chatting and paid her no attention.

"I need you to behave, I need you to stay calm. I'm not going to tranquillise you, because I need you to do something for me. For all of us. Do you understand?"

Selene's eyes roved around under her closed eyelids, and her tongue swept in and out and over her lips.

"We're going to put an end to all of this, to the administration. What you're doing, what you've done already has brought the city to its knees. You're so clever, playing the administration at its own game."

Minnie couldn't be certain, but she thought she saw Selene's mouth curve into a smile. Just for a moment.

"I need you to listen to me. Your daughter is coming. Maeve is coming."

Selene's eyes snapped open, and their focus fell on Minnie's face. Her stare was intense, desperate, and, despite everything they'd believed, very much awake.

"Yes, yes, that's right. Maeve is coming. She's coming to stop all of this. And she's coming to see you."

Minnie raised her hand and stroked Selene's face.

"You know that you can't survive being unplumbed. You know that, don't you?"

Selene blinked and gave just the tiniest nod.

"I'm so sorry. I wish it didn't have to be this way, I wish I could save you. But I can't. Things have gone too far. But you will be able to see your daughter, and hold her. One last time."

Selene nodded again, and her eyes rolled around before coming back to Minnie's. A tear gathered at the corner of one, but didn't fall.

"But Maeve and her friends need help. If they're going to be able to bring down the administration, they need you to help them. So, I'm not going to tranquillise you, but I need you to be quiet and keep still so that everyone believes I have. And I need you to take all of your anger, all of your hatred, and I need you to pour it into the water system. I need you to cause an uprising out there. We need chaos, and you're the only one who can do this. The Daughters will help you, if you pour anger into them too. Rouse them, I know that you can do it."

Selene blinked and nodded again. She licked her lips. "Tell her," she whispered, "tell her that I love her."

Minnie shook her head. "No. You can tell her that yourself."

23

Corinn looked up at the building in front of her. It was featureless; a grey, concrete box. It gave away no secrets, no clues, it simply stood in front of her.

She looked back along the street, along the equally grey and featureless wall that ran the length of it.

Faith had fallen silent some time ago, and Corinn wondered if she knew, somehow, what was going to happen. Even the sky seemed to know; the bright blue replaced by grey clouds that cast shadows over everything.

A short railing in front of her marked the only entrance; a set of stairs leading down to a fortified door underground. Right on cue, the door opened.

Corinn stepped back as two officers emerged. They looked at her and Faith for a moment, as if struggling to even believe they were there.

"You can't be here," the taller of the two said. "This street is restricted."

"I have something to report," Corinn replied coolly.

The officers looked at one another again. Corinn could feel their uncertainty.

"What?"

She sighed, and raised Faith's hand. "This is the girl you've been looking for. The one born to an unmarried woman from The Hope. The one that's been hiding on The Floor."

The officers looked at one another again, frowning.

Corinn shook her head. "Oh, for pity's sake." She closed her eyes and pushed a thought into their heads. There was little else in there to stop it. These men were nothing but uniforms.

They both lifted their guns.

"Oh please, there's no need for that. I'm volunteering her. She's been staying with an elderly lady who lived next door to me. She admitted to me on her death bed who this child really was, and begged me to keep her hidden. But," she shrugged, "that's not really a hassle I need. Obviously she has a real family here somewhere, someone's got to be missing her. So I wanted to do the right thing and bring her back."

The shorter officer stepped forward and took Faith's hand, tugging her hard. Faith tried to cling to Corinn, her fingers scrabbling at her skirt, trying to find a handhold. Corinn glanced down at her, at her damp and pleading eyes.

"You'll have to come with us too," the taller one said. "There's going to be questions."

"I don't think so."

The officers nodded. "We'll be in touch if we

need anything else."

"That's more like it," Corinn replied. She turned and walked away, trying to ignore the sound of Faith crying out her name. She folded her arms and pushed her hands hard into her armpits. Every instinct begged her to turn around, to undo what she'd done, but she buried the urges. She had to see this through. She had to be the monster.

"I'm sorry, Maeve," she whispered to herself. "But I really need you to focus."

24

As she climbed the steps to the refuge, Corinn could hear the hysterics inside. The screaming seeped out from under the door like treacle, it coated the steps like a marsh under Corinn's feet. It grabbed at her ankles, pulled her back, slowed her down.

She grabbed the railing and hauled herself onwards. This had to be done.

The happy ring of the bell as she pushed the door open seemed perverse considering the scene inside.

Corinn couldn't even see Maeve at first, but she could hear her. The wailing was like something unearthly, and it sent a shiver through Corinn's chest. It wasn't a shiver of guilt, simply one of recognition. Of the past catching up to the present and playing itself again.

The sisters were gathered together, heads tucked in, like a mash of clothes and flesh. At the bottom of the mound, Maeve was curled up like a cat, shaking, screaming, clawing at the floor. Every few seconds, a head would bubble out of the pile and scream an order, high-pitched and grating. Women ran around them in a panic. Bringing blankets, water, anything they thought might help to bring calm.

Corinn stepped back as a crowd of them ran outside, calling Faith's name as they went.

She moved further into the café, towards the mound. She cleared her throat.

"You can call off the search parties," she said.

No one even glanced her way.

She sighed. "You can call off the search parties!" she yelled over the noise.

Three fat faces snapped around and stared at her with dark eyes.

A fourth face, red and swollen with tears, emerged from between legs. The curtain of sisters parted, and Maeve crawled out.

"What?" she sobbed.

"What are you doing here?" one of the sisters demanded.

Corinn ignored her and looked straight at Maeve. "You can call off the search parties. Faith isn't missing. She's safe."

"Where is she?" Maeve asked.

"What have you done?" a sister said.

"It's going to hurt now, but in time, you'll see that this is the only way."

"Where is she?" Maeve repeated, lifting herself onto shaky legs. "Where's Faith?"

"I took her to The Compound. I handed her

over to the administration."

The sound that came out of Maeve then was anything but human. It was pure animal instinct, a lioness protecting her cub. She threw herself at Corinn, both feet free of the ground, and when she made contact, she came with teeth and claws.

Corinn fell backwards and Maeve tumbled with her. Blood mingled with tears and sweat and saliva. Thick arms took hold of Maeve, thick fingers clamped around her wrists and dragged her backwards. And all the time, that unearthly noise came from her.

Again, that cold shard of recognition tore through Corinn. She knew that noise. She'd heard it escape from her own mother's mouth. But it hadn't been because of losing Corinn. If she had been loved like that, maybe things could have been different.

"We should let her tear you apart," the sisters hissed.

"How could you?"

"What were you thinking?"

"You are pure evil."

"I'll never see her again," wailed Maeve. She lay, crumpled on the floor like a discarded letter. Like words that wouldn't come easily, a sentiment that couldn't be explained.

Corinn took a deep breath. "You need to listen to me. You will get Faith back, if you listen to me."

Maeve lifted her heavy eyes to Corinn's face.

"I did this because you need to focus, and you can't let yourself be distracted. You need to save the women from The Eye. That's your mission now, your fate. There's never been a better opportunity. If you can save them, then Faith will be returned to you, I promise. You need to do this, Maeve, you need to change everything. For all of us."

Maeve placed her hands on the floor and slowly crawled her way up to standing. She looked as if the slightest breeze would knock her back down, but her face was locked in an expression of determination.

"I will get Faith back," she said. "And after that, I will come for you."

25

Tale pushed the newspaper away. Women weren't supposed to read them, but Colby had accidentally left it out, and she needed to know what was happening.

Their final copy of Asteria had been distributed all over the city. Piles had been left on shop counters, on park benches, they'd been pushed through letter boxes, and passed hand to hand several times over. There would be few people in the city that hadn't seen a copy. The administration wouldn't simply ignore it. They couldn't.

The headline alone had told her everything she wanted to know. It was quite clear: ASTERIA: TERRORIST PROPAGANDA. The article simply went on to say, over and over, that no one should believe what they read and that anyone caught distributing terrorist material would be arrested and dealt with harshly. It was nothing more than sensationalism, hanging on trigger words.

But from what Tale had seen, this newspaper

was too little too late. Anger had taken root in the population, and it was spreading like a contagion. There had been small breakouts of disorder; fights, looting of shops, fire bombs, protests. They had all been dealt with swiftly, but it felt like the beginning of something. The sense of unease was thick in the air, Tale could almost taste it.

But then, this was exactly what they'd wanted. It didn't make it any easier to watch the world go crazy though.

The front door slammed, and Tale jumped. Footsteps charged down the hall before turning into the kitchen. Colby gripped the door frame, his face red and running with sweat.

"What's the matter?" Tale half rose from her chair.

"Thank God, thank God you're here."

"What's happened?"

He gestured for her to sit back down. He gasped, trying to catch his breath.

"I've run all the way back."

"What's happened? You're scaring me."

"I'm sorry, I'm sorry. Some of the guys came to tell me, they saw it on the screen. They were talking about you, Tale, they said you're having a girl."

"What?"

"I know, I can't believe it either. Us, we're going to have a daughter. There's not been a girl born in...I can't even remember how long." He coughed. "But you're in danger. There's been threats made against you. Somehow that terrorist group found out, and they've said they're going to kill you. We have to get you somewhere safe."

"Terrorist group?"

"You know, distributing those lies. Asteron or something."

Tale sighed. "Asteria."

"That's it. We need to get you somewhere safer."

"Colby, I'm not in any danger."

"They don't even know who these people are."

"Trust me, I'm not in any danger."

"Yes, you are, and I'm not going to risk losing you both."

Tale stood and crossed to him. She laid her hand on his heaving shoulder.

"The administration are lying. They're just trying to spread panic, to turn people against Asteria. They're not terrorists, they're the ones telling the truth."

"You haven't been reading their rubbish, have you?"

"Colby, the administration are the liars. I'm not in any danger, believe me."

"You don't know that."

Tale sighed again. "Yes, I do."

"How?"

"Because I wrote it. I'm Asteria."

"What?" He stared at her, his eyes a flow of changing emotions. They reeled across his face clearly, and Tale read each one. Surprise. Confusion. Disbelief. And finally, anger.

"I told you not to get involved, why would you

put yourself in that kind of danger? And our daughter. We're having a girl. You understand how precious that is, don't you?"

"Of course I do," Tale snapped. "I know all about it, far more than you do. Is this the world you want your daughter to grow up in? Taken away from us at sixteen and married off to God knows who? I am fighting for something better for her. What are you doing?"

"What am I doing? I am working my arse off trying to better my position so that, in turn, I can better hers. Just because I'm not a revolutionist doesn't mean I'm not trying to make the world a better place. We don't all need to set the world on fire."

"Well, maybe we should," Tale muttered.

Colby paced the room, dragging his fingers back through his hair.

"Regardless," he said, "what are the administration playing at?"

"They're just trying to discredit Asteria."

"And after that? What do you suppose their next move will be?"

Tale shrugged. "We'll just have to wait and see, I guess."

"I wish we could be a little more prepared. Do you think they know you're involved?"

"How could they?"

"Because they know everything. They have eyes and ears everywhere. Right into our hearts. Sometimes I swear they know what we're going to do before we even know it ourselves."

Tale gave a quick smile and nodded. "That may actually be true."

Colby looked at her with narrowed eyes. "You know something, don't you?"

Tale opened her mouth to answer, but a hammering on the front door stopped her. She pressed her lips together, and looked up at Colby.

"Officers!" came a shout from outside. "Open up!"

"Well," said Tale, "I guess we're about to find out what their next move is."

26

Colby had barely unlatched the front door when the officers came storming in. They looked straight past him to Tale and in just a few strides they had hold of her, pulling her towards the door. She twisted and strained to get loose, but the grip on her was too tight.

"What are you doing?" Colby cried. "Leave her alone, she's pregnant!"

"We're taking her into custody for her own protection. For the protection of the baby."

Colby blocked the doorway, hands on his hips. "You can't take her. That baby is mine too. And she is my wife."

One of the officers stepped forward, standing nose to nose with Colby. He pushed his gun against Colby's chin.

"We have orders to take this woman into custody. No matter what. I will shoot you if you try to stop us."

"No! Colby! Please don't hurt him."

Tale's legs gave out beneath her and she sank

towards the ground. The officers heaved her back up.

"Tale, I'm sorry, I'm so sorry."

Colby reached out for her as she passed, and his fingertips grazed against her cheek. She wished that touch could have lasted forever.

"It's alright, Colby. I'll be alright, I'll be alright."

"I'll get you out, I promise I'll come for you."

As Tale was pushed into the back of a van, she watched Colby racing up the path, arms outstretched, face running with tears. And then the back doors were slammed shut, and he was gone.

27

"Is this it?" Denver asked. He looked around at the small gathering of faces. "Is no one else coming?"

Kerise grimaced. "I guess they're all busy fighting their own little battles now."

"But this is the war," Denver replied. "This is it, this is what their little battles are fighting for. Do they not care?"

Tarin leaned back in his chair and laced his hands behind his head. "Well, I'm glad. I'd much rather work just with people I know and trust." He leaned forward and looked at Maeve. "Except I don't know you."

"This is Maeve," said Kerise.

"Ahh, so you're Maeve." He whispered something into Kerise's ear, and she waved her hands at him.

Denver looked up at Maeve. She was breathing hard, her mouth a sharp line, her eyes even sharper.

"Are you sure you're alright to do this?" he asked. "In the circumstances—"

"I'm fine," Maeve spat, cutting him off. "And I wish you'd all stop asking me. Besides, I've got nothing else to do with my bloody time now, have I?"

"Well, if you're sure."

"Of course I'm sure. You all act like I'm a child who can't possibly know her own mind."

Denver cleared his throat. "I think, before we start talking battle plans, that we need to discuss Tale."

Kerise nodded slowly. "I would presume she's safe enough. She's got a girl inside her, they're not going to risk that baby for anything."

"And what about after she gives birth?"

"All of this will be over by then," Tarin said. "One way or another."

"Do you think—" Denver glanced up at Maeve. "Do you think Selene gave Tale a girl on purpose?"

"Of course she did," said Maeve. "To keep her safe."

"To spur us on," added Kerise.

"It was in the journal," Maeve said softly. She wiped a tear from her cheek. "It was in the journal."

"I don't suppose the journal said whether we were going to win or not," ventured Kerise.

Maeve shook her head and stared at the table.

Denver fought the urge to ask her again if she was alright. He looked around at them all.

"Then we assume Tale's safe for now and figure out what to do about her afterwards? Depending on the outcome?"

Everyone nodded in agreement.

"Right then. I guess it's back to The Eye." He looked at Tarin. "You've been there before, how was it getting in and getting around and stuff?"

"Surprisingly easy. Worryingly so, in fact. But then, it was just me, and I was in an officer's uniform. We'll be going in with a lot more people this time. There's no way we can just storm it. We'll all end up dead. No matter what's going on out there, they'll be defending The Eye right up to the last minute."

"You had help," muttered Maeve.

"What?" said Tarin.

"You had help to get in." She looked up at him. "Corinn helped you. She sent the officers away."

"Are you sure?" Kerise asked.

"Come on, did you really think you were that clever? That sneaky?" She drew the word out mockingly. "Corinn got rid of the guards, she told me she was doing it. So there you have it, we can't do any of this without her. Brilliant. Fantastic."

"Of course we can do it without her," Kerise said.

"No, we can't. You think you're some amazing mercenary or something, Kerise, but you're not. You're just a woman with an axe to grind. Which actually makes you nothing special. You're just the same as every other woman in this shithole of a city." She flicked her hand towards Tarin. "And you, you just got lucky. So if either of you think we can actually do this, you're out of your goddamn minds."

"Then we'll find another way," said Kerise. "Maybe we can ask Selene to help."

"We don't have the time for anymore Chinese whispers," said Tarin. "They're tearing the city apart out there. If we're doing this, it has to be now."

Denver looked around at them. Maeve had deflated them all, ripped the hope out of them. Maybe that's all they'd ever had. Maybe they'd all known it was futile, they'd just refused to accept it.

"If only Freda were here." The words were out before he even realised it.

"There's only one person that can help us, and we all know it." Maeve said.

"Then I guess..." Kerise stopped, and looked at Maeve.

Maeve stood up, knocking her chair over. "No. No way. If you even speak to that evil bitch, then I'm out. I don't want anything to do with her."

Kerise reached out a hand. "Maeve."

"What? What? Would you want to work with her if she'd been the one who took your daughter? To fight alongside her? To trust your life to her?"

No one answered.

"Well then," Maeve said.

They all spun round as the front door of The Paper Duchess opened. The thick smell of smoke poured into the room, and it carried the sound of shouting, gunfire, explosions. It hung in the air above them like a thundercloud, and with it all, with the stench of chaos, came the lightning itself in the form of Corinn.

Maeve crashed around the table and flew at her. The sound that came out of her was one Denver had never heard before, one he hadn't even known was possible, and it cut through everything he thought he knew about the small, slight girl they'd saved from The Floor. The girl he'd thought was so fragile, so incapable. It cut through everything he thought he knew about women, about mothers, about the hearts that beat in their chests.

Tarin was on his feet, his thick hands closing around Maeve's arms, pulling her back. She fought him, thrashing and twisting in his grip, and he struggled to keep hold of her. This huge brute of a man struggled to hold back that waif of a girl.

Corinn sat up and wiped at the blood on her face, smearing it across her lips. Her tongue came out, coating itself in the dark red flux.

"I want to help," she said.

"No," replied Maeve. "No one wants you here."

"You can't do it without me. Let me help."

"We don't need you."

Corinn struggled to her feet and Tarin tightened his grip on Maeve.

"Put your pride away, Maeve. I'm sorry I took Faith, it was a shitty thing to do, but I had no choice. What we're doing, it has to work. I needed you to be focussed. Would you be here right now if you still had Faith? Would you have entrusted her to someone else when they're tearing Falside to pieces?" She wiped her face again. "I want to help. I can get you in there. It's the only way, and you all know it. Use me. Please."

"Why the urgency?" Maeve demanded. "What have you got to gain from this?"

"Other than my freedom?"

"No. Not good enough."

"The world has gone crazy out there. They're wrenching out the door frames of every building. There are people lying dead in the street. You guys started this. You have to finish it too. And you need me to be able to do that."

Kerise looked at Maeve and shrugged.

Maeve shot her hands up. "Whatever," she spat.

As she spoke, one of the windows behind them shattered and glass showered down. A bottle smashed against the floor, its contents bursting into flame. Another followed it, and the room was ablaze in seconds.

"Get out!" screamed Kerise, grabbing hold of Maeve and Corinn.

Tarin raced forward, stamping at some of the flames. He pulled off his jacket and thrashed the fire, trying to extinguish it.

Denver shook his head and grabbed Tarin's arm.

"No," he shouted over the crackle of fire. "No, leave it, let it burn."

They backed away, the heat already feeling like it was blistering their skin.

"Let it burn," he said again.

28

Kerise looked down at the city below them. It was ablaze. There was nothing else to say. Falside was burning.

Along with the flames, came the people. And their anger. And their fists, and their weapons. Crawling up the cliffside like smoke.

But the revolution had already impacted on The Eye. The uniform expanse of lawn was broken here and there by the mound of a body. Some still moving, others lying still. Employees of the administration who had proved themselves to be less than faithful.

Kerise closed her eyes a moment and prayed that Minnie was safe inside.

She looked back at the faces that followed her. Everything now relied on the five of them. As Corinn had said; they had started this, and they needed to finish it. Otherwise, it would finish them.

She gestured to them to follow her, and they set off across the lawn, bent low, heads swinging back and forth, left and right.

Ahead of them, a door slid open, a shard of light cutting across the grass. Boots emerged. Boots and guns. Behind them, the approaching revolution reached The Head.

The two stone lions that guarded the steps were slammed into. Sledgehammers smashed their faces, their muscular flanks, and toppled them from their sentries. People stormed across the grass, brandishing improvised weapons; just items grabbed from their sheds, or their homes. Some came with nothing but their fists and a madness they didn't know how to control.

Kerise looked at her friends. "We need to get inside before this place turns into a battlefield."

"I'll get you in," Corinn said. "I'll move as many guards as I can, but there's a lot of them, and I don't know how long I can hold them off for. You'll have to be quick."

The flash of guns lit the lawn like strobes, making the world around them jar and jolt. Kerise squinted and focussed on the building ahead. It would be too easy to get turned around here, too easy to lose your direction.

Keeping low to the ground, they dashed between the few trees, and behind them, the swell of people came, rising like the tide, ready to drown anyone who got caught in the current.

The officers stormed forward too, but Corinn kept the flow of them away from where the five of them stood.

She flicked her eyes back to Kerise. "I can't concentrate on running and keeping them away from us. I'll have to stay outside."

"No," Kerise said. "We stick together. I can't be responsible for you—"

"You're not," Corinn said, cutting her off. "Whatever happens, it won't be down to you. But I need to concentrate, and I can't do it like this." She grabbed Kerise's hands in hers. "Save those women, get them out of there safely. I'll do what I can."

"We'll see you on the other side of this," Kerise said, squeezing Corinn's fingers tightly. "We wouldn't be able to do this without you."

"Just save them for me."

"We will, and we'll watch the sunrise together, celebrate with a cocktail."

Corinn smiled and nodded; a singular jolt of her head. "Sure we will. Good luck, I know you can do this."

"We have to."

"Yes, you do."

They broke hands, and Corinn stepped around the tree, onto the open lawn. She sat herself down and lifted her eyes to the darkening sky above her. Her hands settled onto the damp grass, and she took a deep breath.

Maeve stepped towards her.

"Thank you for this, Corinn."

Corinn looked up. "I'm sorry I took Faith. You'll understand why I did it."

"I don't know about that. When this is all over...well, we'll see how things turn out."

Corinn nodded and looked back towards the

officers.

"Maeve!" Corinn lurched to the side, shunting Maeve off her feet.

Kerise heard the whistle of the bullet. She heard it penetrate Corinn's chest, and she heard it slam into the tree behind her.

29

Maeve dropped to her knees and stared at the darkening patch on Corinn's jacket, just below her shoulder. She reached out and folded the thick fabric back to reveal the skin underneath. But she couldn't see the skin. She could see blood and tatters of flesh, and it just kept oozing.

Lacing her fingers together, Maeve placed her hands over the hole, and pressed down hard.

"You're going to be ok," she said. "Don't worry, you'll be fine."

"I'll keep the officers back as long as I can," Corinn said.

Kerise nudged Maeve aside, and pressed her own hands against the wound. Denver tugged off his shirt and handed it to Kerise, who packed it under her fists.

Maeve took Corinn's hand in hers.

"I need to tell you something," Corinn said to her.

"It's ok, it's ok."

"No, I need to tell you. My sister. She's one of

the girls in there. That's why I did it. That's why I took Faith. I needed you to be here, to save her."

"Your sister's a psychic too?"

She shook her head quickly. "No. It's me, it was meant to be me. My father hated me and my powers. He was scared of me, of what I could do. Of what I saw inside of him. He was a sick, evil, little man. He was nothing, and a nobody, and the kind of man who would never become anything in life. He hated that. He hated that he was always passed over for promotion, always overlooked. He took his frustrations out on all of us. My mother was almost relieved when he started beating her, because finally something was happening in her life. She had been an ordinary, average child who had grown into a mediocre woman who could only ever dream of being something extraordinary. You know what's really sad? She was jealous of me. She wanted my ability. She'd have happily been led to the gallows for having it. She was desperate for attention, but her whole life, no one had given her more than a second glance." She winced and looked up at Kerise. "You need to go. You need to go now."

"We're not just leaving you," Maeve said. "Kerise, tell her."

Kerise's face darkened. She nodded. "We need to go. While Corinn can still hold the officers back."

Maeve squeezed Corinn's hand hard. "I won't leave you. Tell me about your sister. How did she end up here?"

"My father reported me. She'd overheard them talking about doing it. They were coming to arrest me, but my sister warned me and told me to run. When the officers arrived, they arrested her instead. No matter how much my parents begged and pleaded with them, they wouldn't believe them. They thought they'd simply changed their minds, that they felt too guilty to give up their own daughter." She closed her eyes for a moment. "And they took her away. She's here because of me." She looked back up at Maeve. "So I need you to save her. I need you to make everything right again."

"I will, I promise, and you'll see her soon."

Kerise stood up. The front of her shirt was sodden with blood.

"What are you doing? We're not going to leave her here to bleed to death!" Maeve cried.

"We need to go."

"No!"

"Maeve," Corinn said softly. "If you don't go now, while I can still keep the officers away, all of this will be in vain. And I'll die for nothing."

"You're not going to die."

"Save my sister for me. Go, go. You're mother's waiting to see you."

Reluctantly, Maeve allowed Kerise to pull her to her feet. The ground beneath her had become soft and marshy with the spill of blood, and her skirt was soaked with it.

"Can you forgive me?" asked Corinn.

"Ask me again in the morning." She bent and

kissed Corinn's fingers. "We'll see you soon. We'll save your sister, and then we'll come back for you."

Corinn nodded and managed a weak smile. "Go, now, before it's too late."

Maeve let Kerise pull her away across the lawn, towards The Eye.

30

Inside The Eye, it was cool and quiet. Sterile. Calm. The contrast was almost painful. The functional white walls and stark lighting seemed perverse, as if mocking the scene they had left outside.

Maeve followed blindly, only vaguely aware of Kerise's hand in hers, and the stumbling of her feet along the tiled floor.

Her skirt, heavy with Corinn's blood, clung around her legs, threatening to trip her. It was the weight of Corinn's sacrifice, and Maeve was determined to carry it. She wanted to carry it forever, to make sure no one ever forgot. Whatever happened would be Corinn's legacy. They owed it all to her.

She had been cruel, evil even, but Maeve knew all about desperate situations. She knew about lashing out when you were hurting inside. She knew about having innocent blood on her hands.

The tiles beneath her became metal stairs, and they clattered down into the depths of the building.

The stairwell returned to corridor, and then they stopped.

Finally, Maeve lifted her head and looked around her. Everyone stood silently, facing a set of glass doors.

"Where are they?" whispered Denver.

"In there," Tarin whispered back. "We're here."

"What now?"

The doors slid open and a man and a woman in white coats stepped through. The woman hugged Kerise tightly.

"I was so scared you wouldn't make it through," she said.

"We had a little help. And now we need yours."

"Of course."

Kerise turned to the rest of them. "This is Minnie. This is my daughter."

Minnie tugged her colleague forward. "This is Hector. He's going to be helping us. There was just no way I could do this by myself."

Kerise nodded. "We're grateful to you, Hector."

They all stepped forward into the room beyond, and Maeve's eyes roved over the tangle of pipework that filled the large space. Each pipe was different from the one next to it; the materials and gauges ranging from narrow copper tubes to large plastic ones. They vibrated and rattled, and where they twisted around one another, they trickled and dripped.

"What is this place?" Maeve asked. "Where's my mother?"

Minnie took hold of her sleeve. "You must be

Maeve," she said softly. "Come with me."

They ducked between the pipes, Minnie leading her through a maze she would have become entangled in by herself.

Maeve stopped, and Minnie turned around.

"What is it?"

Curled up amongst the pipes, almost completely concealed by them, was a young woman. She was naked, her head tipped back, her mouth gaping open. She moved slowly, her arms clawing at the air above her as if she were underwater and trying to find the surface. As she turned her head, Maeve gasped. It was Corinn. Or, at least, her sister. They were identical to the smallest detail.

"Twins," Maeve whispered.

"Do you know her?" Minnie asked.

"I know her sister. We can save them, right? We can save all of them?"

Minnie nodded. "The Daughters, yes."

"What about..." She couldn't bring herself to finish the question, but Minnie's face told her what she needed to know.

"Did Kerise not explain that?"

Maeve shook her head.

Minnie took hold of her hand and led her further into the tangle of pipes.

The centre of the room opened up a little. There were fewer pipes here, but they were thicker, and made of iron and concrete. Crouched between them was Maeve's mother.

Maeve rushed forward and cradled her hands

around Selene's face, turning it up towards her. Selene's eyes opened, rested on Maeve, focussed, widened. She raised her arms and patted her hands all over her daughter, as if checking that she were real.

"You're here," she whispered.

"I'm here. I'm here to save you."

"You're here," Selene repeated.

"I'm going to get you out."

Selene shook her head slowly.

"Don't say that," Maeve said. "I came to save you, and I'm not leaving without you."

She looked at the pipes penetrating Selene's body, plumbed in like veins. She wrapped her fingers around one and pulled hard.

"Don't!" cried Minnie.

Selene cried out as the pipe came free.

"You see, we can get you out."

Maeve looked down at her hands, and the torrent of blood streaming over them.

"No, no, no!" She pressed her hands over the flow. "I won't lose you too. I can't."

31

Selene opened her eyes. Pain tore through her body as her energy ebbed. She could feel her life pouring out of her. But she could also feel Maeve. She could feel her hands against her, pressing hard, but she could feel her mind too, the desperation and panic, the horror, the fear. She wouldn't let things end like this.

She reached up into Maeve's head and placed a bud there. She pushed the petals upwards and outwards, encouraged the flower to bloom.

Calm, my daughter, the flower said.

Maeve turned and looked at her.

That's right. I'm here. I love you.

Slowly, a tiny bud opened in Selene's mind. It was shy, tentative, but it bloomed beautifully. Selene closed her eyes and cradled it gently.

Can you hear me? It asked.

I can. I need you to listen to me. There are things you need to know.

The flower in Selene's mind started to close, the petals curling and beginning to brown.

No. You can tell me tomorrow, when all of this is over and we're back together again.

There is no tomorrow for me.

Selene reached out and grabbed Maeve's hands in hers. She squeezed them tightly.

I'm sorry, but this is the way it has to be. This was always how it was going to end.

"No, it doesn't have to be like this," Maeve said aloud.

I need you to understand something. I'm not anything special, I'm not anything extraordinary. These powers they say I have are nothing more than intuition. Nothing more than a talent for reading people. I never had any special abilities. Not until I was pregnant with you.

Selene stroked Maeve's face, and brought her towards her, wrapping her arms tightly around her.

The powers are yours. It was always you.

But I don't have any powers.

You know that you do. But the anger and hatred eats them up. They need the light, the warmth of the sun. You need to forgive Lou for what he did.

Maeve shook her head. *I can't.*

You need to. This is your gift, your strength. Think what you could do with it.

Like Corinn?

Corinn gave into the darkness, she let it change her. But her circle is complete now. Her sister sacrificed herself to save Corinn, and now Corinn has made that sacrifice in return. She's found her peace now.

Maeve lifted her hands and wiped at streams of tears.

You have Faith now, and you must protect her. She's so important, Maeve. One day, she'll lead Falside to true freedom.

"But I need you too. I can't do this alone."

Yes, you can. And I can't stay. I was never meant to. But I am so glad that I got to see you again. My beautiful little girl.

"Please, please. I need you."

Look what you've achieved by yourself. You're so strong, so amazing. And Faith needs you now. She's your future. You need to let go of the past. Let go of me.

"I can't. I've only just got you back."

Get rid of the journal. Promise me. It's no help to you now. You have an entire future to build.

Maeve nodded as tears poured down her face.

Selene's arms dropped from around her. She no longer had the strength to cling on. The flower she'd placed in Maeve's head began to close, and she couldn't open it again.

I love you.

"No! Don't you die!"

I need you to save the other women. I've made sure now that they'll live.

"No!"

Selene watched Maeve's tears fall against her skin, but she couldn't feel them. She closed her eyes.

I am so proud of you.

32

Hector grabbed Kerise's arm, pushing packets of synthetic skin into her hands.

"You need to patch these over everywhere you pull a pipe from. The Daughters aren't plumbed in like the Mother. There'll be blood, but not too much."

"So, we can save them all?"

Hector nodded. "There's no reason why we can't, as long as we can get them straight out of here and somewhere with better medical supplies." He looked up towards the centre of the room. "It's only..."

"I know. Poor Maeve."

"Come on, we need to hurry." He handed more packets to Denver. "God only knows what's going on out there, we could have an army come running through those doors any minute."

Kerise clambered through the tangle of pipes towards the sound of whimpering. The Daughters were waking up.

She spotted a foot, kicking against the

pipework.

"My God." Kneeling down, she pushed back the flow of dark hair to reveal Corinn's face underneath.

Her hands shook as she clumsily pulled open the first skin packet.

"I knew your sister," she said.

The Daughter looked up at her, her bleary eyes beginning to sharpen.

"Corinn," the Daughter whispered.

"Yes, Corinn. She did a brave thing tonight, and if it wasn't for her, we wouldn't be rescuing you now."

"Corinn," she said again.

She winced as Kerise pulled a pipe out of her. It was buried deep, and was slick with blood. Kerise pressed the synthetic skin over the wound, and it clung tightly.

"A lot of people will have things to say about your sister, but you need to remember, she sacrificed herself to save everyone. She's a hero, never forget that."

"Corinn."

33

Warm hands slipped themselves around Maeve and lifted her from the cold body of Selene. She tried to cling on, but she had no energy to fight anymore.

Somewhere she could hear explosions, shouting. A blast of heat hit her skin, and then the cool air outside.

She closed her eyes.

34

Tale joined Denver and took hold of his hand. She looked up at the burnt out shell of The Paper Duchess.

"Are you going to rebuild her?" she asked.

"Can't afford to. No, let her stand as a reminder of what happened."

"I never did know. Why 'The Paper Duchess'?"

Denver grinned. "In honour of my mother. So proud, so full of her own importance, but hold a light up to her, and you can see right through."

"This is where we met. Do you remember?"

Denver nodded. "Freda brought you. You were clumsy, awkward, shy. I thought you'd be gone within a week. I certainly couldn't see what Freda saw in you."

"Well, you were so in love with her back then."

Denver snorted. "More fool me."

"Do you think we'll see her again?"

"I do. I really do."

"There's women pouring out of the city now. I guess they just want to taste a bit of freedom."

"I guess so. There's a whole world out there to explore now. Are you not tempted?"

Tale patted her stomach. "I'm not really up for much travelling at the moment."

"I guess not."

"They opened up the borders pretty quickly."

"I don't think they had much choice. Most of the checkpoints had been torn down in the riots anyway. But with the administration in tatters, they couldn't hold onto that sort of control anymore. The leaders were murdered, half of the officers had joined the revolution. The old regime had to be removed completely."

"And now we have the promise of elections. For the first time in almost a century."

"Democracy," Denver said with a nod.

"It's going to be weird."

"Yes, but it's better than a temporary military rule. This uncertainty is uncomfortable. No one really knows what to do with themselves. Democracy will be good. That is, as long as it's handled properly. I suspect, whoever wins, there's going to be calls of foul play."

"You're probably right. People are suspicious of new things."

"Even when it benefits them."

Tale smiled grimly. "We don't know that it will yet. We could be entering a whole new era of hell."

Denver squeezed her hand. "It'll all work out."

"How can you be so sure?"

"Because, otherwise, what we did will be for nothing. And I can't let myself believe that."

"How is your leg now?"

"On the mend. The bullet went straight through. I was lucky, really."

"Unlike Corinn."

Denver nodded. "Unlike Corinn."

"I just hope she'll be remembered kindly."

"We'll make sure she is."

"How's her sister doing?"

Denver shrugged. "We took her home, and her parents are looking after her now."

"Filling her head with stories of Corinn, no doubt."

"They were scared of her, but it doesn't mean they didn't love her. They were distraught when Kerise told them."

Tale sighed and placed her hand on the curve of her belly. "What are you going to do now?"

Denver grinned. "Maybe I'll stand in the elections. What do you think?"

"Well, you were one of the team that brought down the administration. You're a hero."

"Not that anyone even knows."

"Bitter that you're missing out on all the glory?"

"I was hoping for some kind of parade in our honour, yes."

Tale laughed. "Sorry, but you're destined to be completely forgotten by history."

"Story of my life. And what about you? What are you going to do?"

"Me?" She smiled. "I'm going to go home."

35

Maeve slammed her hands down on the reception desk and the young officer behind it jumped.

"I'm back. Again."

"Erm...erm...what name was it?"

"Faith Richards. She's the little girl. The one you're keeping wrongfully imprisoned. You'll find her name on the list of people due to be released since the collapse of the administration."

The officer picked up his screen, almost dropped it, and scrolled through the list.

"She's not here, I'm sorry. If you come back—"

"No, no, not 'if I come back'. I've been coming back for five days now. She was arrested under administration laws, laws that are now overturned. She's being wrongfully held. She's only four years old."

"I'm sorry, the backlog of cases to be reassessed is huge. They're working through them as fast as they can."

"Don't fob me off with stories of bureaucracy. That's not my problem."

The officer waved his screen at her. "She's not on my list, I'm sorry. I just don't have the authority to—"

"Then find somebody who does, not just a boy in a uniform."

Maeve jumped as a hand rested on her shoulder. She turned and met the eyes of her father. She looked him up and down and grinned. He was stood, chin lifted high, in his monk's robes. They were nothing but a costume now; he hadn't been allowed to return to his former role.

"You heard her," he said. "Go and find your superior, or their superior, or *their* superior. I don't care if you have to go all the way to the top to sort this out. That girl is coming home today, list or no list. You have no right to keep her." He stepped past Maeve and leant over the desk, placing his nose almost tip to tip with the officer's. "Or do you want to answer to the ultimate authority?"

The officer almost fell out of his chair in his scrabble to get to his feet. He backed out of the room with a whimper.

Maeve looked at Harris. "Isn't it illegal to impersonate a monk?"

Harris shrugged. "Did I say that I was a monk? I just like these clothes. Nice and airy."

"Thank you for coming."

"Don't mention it."

"I have to get her back. She must be so scared."

Harris took hold of her hand and squeezed it. "Everything's going to be fine. You'll see."

"Everyone keeps saying that. And there's been so many times when I've finally thought 'this is it. Now it's all over.' But then something else happens, and it seems like there's always another battle to fight."

"This is your last one, I promise."

Maeve shook her head. "I still have to get them to release Mum's body."

"Leave that to me. I'll take care of everything."

Maeve nodded. "Thank you, that would be a relief. I really need to concentrate on Faith right now. The rest of the world can sort itself out."

"So you're done with being a revolutionist?"

"For now at least. I just want a nice, normal, quiet life. Is that too much to ask?"

"It might be, considering your parentage."

Maeve huffed. "Always one more drama, eh?"

"C'mon, what else would you do with your time?"

Maeve raised her eyebrows in reply.

"So what are you going to do now? Once you have Faith back?"

"Go home. Sleep in my own bed. Watch the future unfold."

"You're not considering standing in the election then?"

"Are you?"

Harris laughed loudly. "I think a slum girl might have even more chance of getting elected than a disgraced monk. If only I knew where my own bed might be."

"There's room for another one at our house. It

would be nice for Faith to have her grandfather close by."

"Do you mean it?"

"Yes, I do. I'd really like it if you moved in."

Harris smiled broadly, and looked away. "You're stuck with me then."

Maeve gave him a playful nudge. "I think I can live with that."

"I'll ask you again after you've suffered a week of me snoring and farting."

The door at the back of the room finally reopened, and the young officer hurried through. He glanced at Harris, but spoke directly to Maeve.

"I'm sorry for the inconvenience, it was a simple clerical error, and we apologise for that. Your daughter can return with you today."

Maeve clamped her hand over her mouth as the sobs pushed their way up her throat. The tears came suddenly; a sheen of joy across her skin. Harris' arms closed around her, pulling her tight against him.

"This is your last battle won," he whispered. "This is your victory."

Maeve broke free of Harris' embrace as Faith came through the door. She stopped and stared for a moment, before running, full speed, into Maeve's waiting arms.

Maeve scooped her up and covered her face in tears and kisses.

"I'll never let you go again," she said.

36

Tale stopped and bent into the pram, unable to resist the warm plumpness of that tiny cheek, and the feather-like softness of those curls. She wanted to scoop her up and hold her tightly forever, but she equally wanted to watch her sleep blissfully.

She trundled forward again, frowning at the unevenness of the pavement, terrified that this moment might disappear, be stolen away by the corner of a drain.

But it wasn't a drain that the pram struck, it was a woman. A woman with red hair that glowed in the sunlight.

Tale's mouth dropped open, and her hands fell from the handle of the pram. She stepped backwards, fighting to find her voice.

"Hi," Freda said.

"Hi," Tale repeated. Her mind felt suddenly empty of vocabulary; nothing but a void where there were once words and sentences. She opened her mouth again, but closed it for fear of what might pour out.

"I'm sorry to catch you by surprise," said Freda.

Tale nodded dumbly.

"May I?" She gestured towards the pram.

Tale nodded again.

Freda moved around to the side of it, and peered under the hood. "Oh, she's beautiful, Tale. She looks just like you."

Tale lifted her hand, pressing her fingers against Freda's shoulder before she even realised that she was moving.

"It really is you," she said. "You really are here."

Freda took hold of Tale's hand and placed it against her cheek. "It really is me."

"Then all of this really is over. At last."

"It's a shock when the world turns upside-down, right? Even if it is what you always wanted to happen."

"I've been so wrapped up in this little one that, honestly, I've barely noticed. I've been living in a bit of a bubble, I guess."

"Who wouldn't?" Freda looked back into the pram.

Tale's brain switched back on, and the jolt of it almost made her jump.

"I'm sorry, I'm on my way to meet up with the others. They would love to see you, and they'll be so shocked. And maybe I won't feel like the only idiot around here gaping like a fish."

"That would be really good. I've literally only just arrived back in Falside. I was on my way to the

Duchess anyway."

"Oh, we're not meeting there. The Duchess kind of got burnt down."

"What? Really?"

Tale nodded.

"How's Denver coping with it?"

Tale thought for a moment and then smiled. "Philosophically."

Freda grinned. "Typical Denver. It's nice to know that some things don't change."

"A lot has changed though."

"Of course, you're a wife now, and a mother."

"He's a kind man, Freda, and he's good to me. He really loves me."

"Do you love him?"

Tale inhaled deeply, letting the breath trail slowly back out. She nodded quickly. "I really think I do."

Freda smiled and nodded in return. "Good. I'm happy for you."

"Really?"

"Of course. I couldn't expect...I mean...your daughter's going to have one kick-ass auntie."

Tale reached out and squeezed Freda's hand. "I'd like that."

The bell above the refuge door tingled merrily as Freda held it open. Tale pushed the pram inside, wincing as she crashed it into numerous chairs and tables.

"Looks like you need learner plates on that thing," Denver said, jumping up to help her.

"I really do," replied Tale.

With a chair lifted halfway, Denver stopped, and stared. He slowly lowered the chair.

"Is this a ghost?" he said.

Freda stepped forward into the café, letting the door close behind her.

"No, it's really me."

In two strides he was across the room, and she was in his arms. He buried his face into her neck as his body convulsed with tears. Kerise was on her feet too, her arms wrapped around them, until they were just a mass of people, and it was impossible to tell where one of them ended and the next began.

Tale smiled. She searched for a shred of jealousy inside her, looked deep for bitterness or regret, but she found none. Just happiness, and the feeling that everything really was going to be alright. Just like everyone always promised regardless of whether they believed it or not.

She looked over at Maeve, and Faith on her knee. She looked at Tarin, Minnie, and Hector leaning against the counter, sharing a joke. She looked at Harris stood the other side of it, arms folded, watching his daughter and granddaughter. She looked at Corinn's sister, Leta, who was growing in strength and confidence every day. And she knew that, no matter what happened, they'd survive. Because they had to. Because they believed in the future, and they were willing to fight for it.

Kerise, Denver, and Freda joined the rest of

them, their eyes raw with tears.

Harris brought a tray of drinks to the table, and they all leaned in and took one.

Kerise held her glass up and cleared her throat.

"A toast, I certainly think we deserve it. We may not be heroes to the city, and we may not be remembered in the history books, but each and every one of you is a hero. Falside still stands today, all be it broken and unsure of itself, but it still stands because of us and what we did. Every one of us here sacrificed something or someone to create a future that we can be proud of. A future that now belongs to our legacies, our children, Faith and..." She looked at Tale. "Has that poor child got a name yet?"

Tale looked over at Maeve. "I thought that maybe I'd call her Selene. If that's alright."

Maeve nodded. "That's definitely ok." She looked up at Harris and they exchanged smiles.

"Ok then," continued Kerise, "Faith and little Selene. They are the ones who will shape Falside and whatever it becomes. And it is for them, ultimately, that we fought the fight that we did. As in any battle, not everyone was able to come home, and the ultimate sacrifice paid by Selene," Kerise nodded at Maeve, "and Corinn," she nodded at Leta, "will never be forgotten. As long as we have breath in our bodies, we will tell their stories, and speak their names to anyone who will listen."

"And even those who won't," added Tarin.

"Absolutely. And these two girls will know their

stories, and, someday in the future, they will tell the stories to their daughters, and their granddaughters, and their great-granddaughters."

"Here, here," called Harris.

"And they will live forever, long after all of us have become nothing but worm food." Kerise smiled. "And so, the toast, to each and every one of us, because we are amazing and awesome as individuals, but together we're unstoppable."

The glasses clanked together, and the drink sloshed out over knuckles and gathered in pools on the table.

EPILOGUE

Maeve placed the journal on the surface of the water, holding it against the current with one hand. With the other, she placed a rose on its cover. And then she let it go.

With her bare feet buried into the silt of the riverbed, the water pulling at her skirt, she watched the journal float away, spinning around, rising and falling.

She looked back towards the shore where Harris stood, Faith's hand gripped in his.

Bunching her sodden skirt into her fists, she waded back towards them, and up out of the river.

Harris hugged her with his free arm.

"You ok?" he asked.

Maeve nodded. "Actually, yes. It feels kind of freeing. And it was a promise. It feels good to have fulfilled that."

"They're releasing her body today."

Maeve sighed. "Finally."

"I thought we'd choose a cemetery outside the city for her."

"Give her her freedom."

Harris nodded. "Exactly right."

"I think it's a lovely idea." Maeve lifted Faith up onto her hip. "Let's go home."

ABOUT ANGELINE TREVENA

Angeline Trevena was born and bred in a rural corner of Devon, but now lives among the breweries and canals of central England with her husband, their two sons, and a rather neurotic cat. She is a horror and fantasy writer, poet, and journalist.

In 2003 she graduated from Edge Hill University, Lancashire, with a BA Hons Degree in Drama and Writing. During this time she decided that her future lay in writing words rather than performing them.

Some years ago she worked at an antique auction house and religiously checked every wardrobe that came in to see if Narnia was in the back of it. She's still not given up looking for it.

Find out more at www.angelinetrevena.co.uk

ACKNOWLEDGEMENTS

I've thought a lot about what to write here. And every time I've come up with a blank. I can't find words that are grand enough for such a momentous moment, yet, at the same time, humble and thankful enough for all of the people who have helped me get to this point.

My husband, who keeps my feet on the ground, and stops me from floating away entirely. He's also the best alpha reader anyone could wish for, making coffee shop plotting sessions such a joy that they're over far too soon. My two wonderful, beautiful boys who are my entire world. They may be frustrating distractions at times, but my whole being is richer for having them.

My little brother, Ben, and his wonderfully creepy miniature models that have adorned the covers of the whole series. You're a nerdy genius, a geeky miracle-maker.

My parents who have championed me the whole way. All I've ever wanted is to make you guys proud of me, and I really hope I have.

All of my beta readers, editors, and proofreaders along the way: Heidi, Anthony, Tony, Pixie, Sara. Your critical eyes and honest feedback have been invaluable. You're all wonderful in both your generous praise and your honourable brutality.

And everyone else who has cheered me on, and read my stories, and been absolutely amazing.